She hurried to Timmie, who clung to her, curling his little bandy legs—still thin, so thin—about her.

Hoskins watched, then said gravely, "He seems quite unhappy."

Miss Fellowes said, "I don't blame him. They're at him every day now with their blood samples and their probings. They keep him on synthetic diets that I wouldn't feed a pig."

"It's the sort of thing they can't try on a human, you know."

"They can't try it on Timmie either. After he's had a bad session with them, he has nightmares, he can't sleep. NOW I WARN YOU" (she reached a sudden peak of fury) "I'm not letting them in here any more."

The Tor Double Novels

ISAAC ASIMOV
THE UGLY LITTLE BOY

A TOM DOHERTY ASSOCIATES BOOK
NEW YORK

EDITH FELLOWES SMOOTHED her working smock as she always did before opening the elaborately locked door and stepping across the invisible dividing line between the *is* and the *is not*. She carried her notebook and her pen although she no longer took notes except when she felt the absolute need for some report.

This time she also carried a suitcase. ("Games for the boy," she had said, smiling, to the guard—who had long since stopped even thinking of questioning her and who waved her on.)

And, as always, the ugly little boy knew that she had entered and came running to her, crying, "Miss Fellowes—Miss Fellowes——" in his soft, slurring way.

"Timmie," she said, and passed her hand over the shaggy, brown hair on his misshapen little head. "What's wrong?"

He said, "Will Jerry be back to play again? I'm sorry about what happened."

"Never mind that now, Timmie. Is that why you've been crying?"

He looked away. "Not just about that, Miss Fellowes. I dreamed again."

"The same dream?" Miss Fellowes' lips set.

Of course, the Jerry affair would bring back the dream.

He nodded. His too large teeth showed as he tried to smile and the lips of his forward-thrusting mouth stretched wide. "When will I be big enough to go out there, Miss Fellowes?"

"Soon," she said softly, feeling her heart break. "Soon."

Miss Fellowes let him take her hand and enjoyed the warm touch of the thick dry skin of his palm. He led her through the three rooms that made up the whole of Stasis Section One—comfortable enough, yes, but an eternal prison for the ugly little boy all the seven (was it seven?) years of his life.

He led her to the one window, looking out onto a scrubby woodland section of the world of *is* (now hidden by night), where a fence and painted instructions allowed no men to wander without permission.

He pressed his nose against the window. "Out there, Miss Fellowes?"

"Better places. Nicer places," she said sadly as she looked at his poor little imprisoned face outlined in profile against the window. The forehead retreated flatly and his hair lay down in tufts upon it. The back of his skull bulged and seemed to make the head overheavy so that it sagged and bent forward, forcing the whole body into a stoop. Already, bony ridges were beginning to bulge the skin above his eyes. His wide mouth thrust forward more prominently than did his wide and flattened nose and he had no chin to speak of, only a jawbone that curved smoothly down and back. He was small for his years and his stumpy legs were bowed.

He was a very ugly little boy and Edith Fellowes loved him dearly.

Her own face was behind his line of vision, so she allowed her lips the luxury of a tremor.

They would *not* kill him. She would do anything to prevent it. Anything. She opened the suitcase and began taking out the clothes it contained.

Edith Fellowes had crossed the threshold of Stasis, Inc. for the first time just a little over three years before. She hadn't, at that time, the slightest idea as to what Stasis meant or what the place did. No one did then, except those who worked there. In fact, it was only the day after she arrived that the news broke upon the world.

At the time, it was just that they had advertised for a woman with knowledge of physiology, experience with clinical chemistry, and a love for children. Edith Fellowes had been a nurse in a maternity ward and believed she fulfilled those qualifications.

Gerald Hoskins, whose name plate on the desk included a Ph.D. after the name, scratched his cheek with his thumb and looked at her steadily.

Miss Fellowes automatically stiffened and felt her face (with its slightly asymmetric nose and its a-trifle-too-heavy eyebrows) twitch.

He's no dreamboat himself, she thought resentfully. He's getting fat and bald and he's got a sullen mouth. ——But the salary mentioned had been considerably higher than she had expected, so she waited.

Hoskins said, "Now do you really love children?"

"I wouldn't say I did if I didn't."

"Or do you just love pretty children? Nice chubby children with cute little button-noses and gurgly ways?"

Miss Fellowes said, "Children are children, Dr. Hoskins, and the ones that aren't pretty are just the ones who may happen to need help most."

"Then suppose we take you on——"

"You mean you're offering me the job now?"

He smiled briefly, and for a moment, his broad face had an absentminded charm about it. He said, "I make quick decisions. So far the offer is tentative, however. I may make as quick a decision to let you go. Are you ready to take the chance?"

Miss Fellowes clutched at her purse and calculated just as swiftly as she could, then ignored calculations and followed impulse. "All right."

"Fine. We're going to form the Stasis tonight and I think you had better be there to take over at once. That will be at 8 P.M. and I'd appreciate it if you could be here at 7:30."

"But what——"

"Fine. Fine. That will be all now." On signal, a smiling secretary came in to usher her out.

Miss Fellowes stared back at Dr. Hoskins' closed door for a moment. What was Stasis? What had this large barn of a building—with its badged employees, its makeshift corridors, and its unmistakable air of engineering—to do with children?

She wondered if she should go back that evening or stay away and teach that arrogant man a lesson. But she knew she would be back if only out of sheer frustration. She would have to find out about the children.

She came back at 7:30 and did not have to announce herself. One after another, men and women seemed to know her and to know her function. She found herself all but placed on skids as she was moved inward.

Dr. Hoskins was there, but he only looked at her distantly and murmured, "Miss Fellowes."

He did not even suggest that she take a seat, but she drew one calmly up to the railing and sat down.

They were on a balcony, looking down into a large pit, filled with instruments that looked like a cross between the control panel of a spaceship and the working face of a computer. On one side were partitions that seemed to make up an unceilinged apartment, a giant dollhouse into the rooms of which she could look from above.

She could see an electronic cooker and a freeze-space unit in one room and a washroom arrangement off another. And surely the object she made out in another room could only be part of a bed, a small bed.

Hoskins was speaking to another man and, with Miss Fellowes, they made up the total occupancy of the balcony. Hoskins did not offer to introduce the other man, and Miss Fellowes eyed him surreptitiously. He was thin and quite fine-looking in a middle-aged way. He had a small mustache and keen eyes that seemed to busy themselves with everything.

He was saying, "I won't pretend for one moment that I understand all this, Dr. Hoskins; I mean, except as a layman, a reasonably intelligent laymen, may be expected to understand it. Still, if there's one part I understand less than another, it's this matter of selectivity. You can only reach out so far; that seems sensible; things get dimmer the further you go; it takes more energy.——But then, you can only reach out so near. That's the puzzling part."

"I can make it seem less paradoxical, Deveney, if you will allow me to use an analogy."

(Miss Fellowes placed the new man the moment she heard his name, and despite herself was impressed. This was obviously Candide Deveney, the science writer of the Telenews, who was notoriously at the scene of every major scientific break-through. She even recognized his face as one she saw on the news-plate when the landing on Mars had been announced. ——So Dr. Hoskins must have something important here.

"By all means use an analogy," said Deveney ruefully, "if you think it will help."

"Well, then, you can't read a book with ordinary-sized print if it is held six feet from your eyes, but you can read it if you hold it one foot from your eyes. So far, the closer the better. If you bring the book to within one inch of your eyes, however, you've lost it again. There is such a thing as being too close, you see."

"Hmm," said Deveney.

"Or take another example. Your right shoulder is about thirty inches from the tip of your right forefinger and you can place your right forefinger on your right shoulder. Your right elbow is only half the distance from the tip of your right forefinger; it should by all ordinary logic be easier to reach, and yet you cannot place your right finger on your right elbow. Again, there is such a thing as being too close."

Deveney said, "May I use these analogies in my story?"

"Well, of course. Only too glad. I've been waiting long enough for someone like you to have a story. I'll give you anything else you want. It is time, finally, that we want the world looking over our shoulder. They'll see something."

(Miss Fellowes found herself admiring his calm certainty despite herself. There was strength there.)

Deveney said, "How far out will you reach?"

"Forty thousand years."

Miss Fellowes drew in her breath sharply.

Years?

There was tension in the air. The men at the controls scarcely moved. One man at a microphone spoke into it in a soft monotone, in short phrases that made no sense to Miss Fellowes.

Deveney, leaning over the balcony railing with an intent stare, said, "Will we see anything, Dr. Hoskins?"

"What? No. Nothing till the job is done. We detect indirectly, something on the principle of radar, except that we use mesons rather than radiation. Mesons reach backward under the proper conditions. Some are reflected and we must analyze the reflections."

"That sounds difficult."

Hoskins smiled again, briefly as always. "It is the end product of fifty years of research; forty years of it before I entered the field. ——Yes, it's difficult."

The man at the microphone raised one hand.

Hoskins said, "We've had the fix on one particular moment in time for weeks, breaking it, remaking it after calculating our own movements in time; making certain that we could handle time-flow with sufficient precision. This must work now."

But his forehead glistened.

Edith Fellowes found herself out of her seat and at the balcony railing, but there was nothing to see.

The man at the microphone said quietly, "Now."

There was a space of silence sufficient for one breath and then the sound of a terrified little boy's scream from the dollhouse rooms. Terror! Piercing terror!

Miss Fellowes' head twisted in the direction of the cry. A child was involved. She had forgotten.

And Hoskins' fist pounded on the railing and he said in a tight voice, trembling with triumph, "*Did* it."

Miss Fellowes was urged down the short, spiral flight of steps by the hard press of Hoskins' palm between her shoulder blades. He did not speak to her.

The men who had been at the controls were standing about now, smiling, smoking, watching the three as they entered on the main floor. A very soft buzz sounded from the direction of the dollhouse.

Hoskins said to Deveney, "It's perfectly safe to enter Stasis. I've done it a thousand times. There's a queer sensation which is momentary and means nothing."

He stepped through an open door in mute demonstration, and Deveney, smiling stiffly and drawing an obviously deep breath, followed him.

Hoskins said, "Miss Fellowes! Please!" He crooked his forefinger impatiently.

Miss Fellowes nodded and stepped stiffly through. It was as though a ripple went through her, an internal tickle.

But once inside all seemed normal. There was the smell of the fresh wood of the dollhouse and—of—of soil somehow.

There was silence now, no voice at last, but there was the dry shuffling of feet, a scrabbling as of a hand over wood—then a low moan.

"Where is it?" asked Miss Fellowes in distress. Didn't these fool men *care?*

The boy was in the bedroom; at least the room with the bed in it.

It was standing naked, with its small, dirt-smeared chest heaving raggedly. A bushel of dirt and coarse grass spread over the floor at his bare brown feet. The smell of soil came from it and a touch of something fetid.

Hoskins followed her horrified glance and said with annoyance, "You can't pluck a boy cleanly out of time, Miss Fellowes. We had to take some of the surroundings with it for safety.

Or would you have preferred to have it arrive here minus a leg or with only half a head?"

"Please!" said Miss Fellowes, in an agony of revulsion. "Are we just to stand here? The poor child is frightened. And it's *filthy*."

She was quite correct. It was smeared with encrusted dirt and grease and had a scratch on its thigh that looked red and sore.

As Hoskins approached him, the boy, who seemed to be something over three years in age, hunched low and backed away rapidly. He lifted his upper lip and snarled in a hissing fashion like a cat. With a rapid gesture, Hoskins seized both the child's arms and lifted him, writhing and screaming, from the floor.

Miss Fellowes said, "Hold him, now. He needs a warm bath first. He needs to be cleaned. Have you the equipment? If so, have it brought here, and I'll need to have help in handling him just at first. Then, too, for heaven's sake, have all this trash and filth removed."

She was giving the orders now and she felt perfectly good about that. And because now she was an efficient nurse, rather than a confused spectator, she looked at the child with a clinical eye—and hesitated for one shocked moment. She saw past the dirt and shrieking, past the thrashing of limbs and useless twisting. She saw the boy himself.

It was the ugliest little boy she had ever seen. It was horribly ugly from misshapen head to bandy legs.

She got the boy cleaned with three men helping her and with others milling about in their efforts to clean the room. She worked in silence and with a sense of outrage, annoyed by the continued strugglings and outcries of the boy and by the undignified drenchings of soapy water to which she was subjected.

Dr. Hoskins had hinted that the child would not be pretty, but that was far from stating that it would be repulsively deformed. And there was a stench about the boy that soap and water was only alleviating little by little.

She had the strong desire to thrust the boy, soaped as he was, into Hoskins' arms and walk out; but there was the pride of profession. She had accepted an assignment, after all. ——And there would be the look in his eyes. A cold look that would read: Only pretty children, Miss Fellowes?

He was standing apart from them, watching coolly from a distance with a half-smile on his face when he caught her eyes, as though amused at her outrage.

She decided she would wait a while before quitting. To do so now would only demean her.

Then, when the boy was a bearable pink and smelled of scented soap, she felt better anyway. His cries changed to whimpers of exhaustion as he watched carefully, eyes moving in quick frightened suspicion from one to another of those in the room. His cleanness accentuated his thin nakedness as he shivered with cold after his bath.

Miss Fellowes said sharply, "Bring me a nightgown for the child!"

A nightgown appeared at once. It was as

though everything were ready and yet nothing were ready unless she gave orders; as though they were deliberately leaving this in her charge without help, to test her.

The newsman, Deveney, approached and said, "I'll hold him, Miss. You won't get it on by yourself."

"Thank you," said Miss Fellowes. And it was a battle indeed, but the nightgown went on, and when the boy made as though to rip it off, she slapped his hand sharply.

The boy reddened, but did not cry. He stared at her and the splayed fingers of one hand moved slowly acrosss the flannel of the night-gown, feeling the strangeness of it.

Miss Fellowes thought desperately: Well, what next?

Everyone seemed in suspended animation, waiting for her—even the ugly little boy.

Miss Fellowes said sharply, "Have you provided food? Milk?"

They had. A mobile unit was wheeled in, with its refrigeration compartment containing three quarts of milk, with a warming unit and a supply of fortifications in the form of vitamin drops, copper-cobalt-iron syrup and others she had no time to be concerned with. There was a variety of canned self-warming junior foods.

She used milk, simply milk, to begin with. The radar unit heated the milk to a set temperature in a matter of ten seconds and clicked off, and she put some in a saucer. She had a certainty about the boy's savagery. He wouldn't know how to handle a cup.

Miss Fellowes nodded and said to the boy,

"Drink. Drink." She made a gesture as though to raise the milk to her mouth. The boy's eyes followed but he made no move.

Suddenly, the nurse resorted to direct measures. She seized the boy's upper arm in one hand and dipped the other in the milk. She dashed the milk across his lips, so that it dripped down cheeks and receding chin.

For a moment, the child uttered a high-pitched cry, then his tongue moved over his wetted lips. Miss Fellowes stepped back.

The boy approached the saucer, bent toward it, then looked up and behind sharply as though expecting a crouching enemy; bent again and licked at the milk eagerly, like a cat. He made a slurping noise. He did not use his hands to lift the saucer.

Miss Fellowes allowed a bit of the revulsion she felt show on her face. She couldn't help it.

Deveney caught that, perhaps. He said, "Does the nurse know, Dr. Hoskins?"

"Know what?" demanded Miss Fellowes.

Deveney hesitated, but Hoskins (again that look of detached amusement on his face) said, "Well, tell her."

Deveney addressed Miss Fellowes. "You may not supect it, Miss, but you happen to be the first civilized woman in history ever to be taking care of a Neanderthal youngster."

She turned on Hoskins with a kind of controlled ferocity. "You might have told me, Doctor."

"Why? What difference does it make?"

"You said a child."

"Isn't that a child? Have you ever had a
puppy or a kitten, Miss Fellowes? Are those
closer to the human? If that were a baby chim-
panzee, would you be repelled? You're a nurse,
Miss Fellowes. Your record places you in a maternity ward for three years. Have you ever refused to take care of a deformed infant?"

Miss Fellowes felt her case slipping away. She
said, with much less decision, "You might have
told me."

"And you would have refused the position?
Well, do you refuse it now?" He gazed at her
coolly, while Deveney watched from the other
side of the room, and the Neanderthal child,
having finished the milk and licked the plate,
looked up at her with a wet face and wide, long-
ing eyes.

The boy pointed to the milk and suddenly
burst out in a short series of sounds repeated
over and over; sounds made up of gutturals and
elaborate tongue-clickings.

Miss Fellowes said, in surprise, "Why, he talks."

"Of course," said Hoskins. "Homo neanderthalensis is not a truly separate species, but rather
a subspecies of Homo sapiens. Why shouldn't he
talk? He's probably asking for more milk."

Automatically, Miss Fellowes reached for the
bottle of milk, but Hoskins seized her wrist.
"No, Miss Fellowes, before we go any further,
are you staying on the job?"

Miss Fellowes shook free in annoyance,
"Won't you feed him if I don't? I'll stay with
him—for a while."

She poured the milk.

Hoskins said, "We are going to leave you with

the boy, Miss Fellowes. This is the only door to Stasis Number One and it is elaborately locked and guarded. I'll want you to learn the details of the lock which will, of course, be keyed to your fingerprints as they are already keyed to mine. The spaces overhead" (he looked upward to the open ceilings of the dollhouse) "are also guarded and we will be warned if anything untoward takes place in here."

Miss Fellowes said indignantly, "You mean I'll be under view." She thought suddenly of her own survey of the room interiors from the balcony.

"No, no," said Hoskins seriously, "your privacy will be respected completely. The view will consist of electronic symbolism only, which only a computer will deal with. Now you will stay with him tonight, Miss Fellowes, and every night until further notice. You will be relieved during the day according to some schedule you will find convenient. We will allow you to arrange that."

Miss Fellowes looked about the dolhouse with a puzzled expression. "But why all this, Dr. Hoskins? Is the boy dangerous?"

"It's a matter of energy, Miss Fellowes. He must never be allowed to leave these rooms. Never. Not for an instant. Not for any reason. Not to save his life. Not even to save *your* life, Miss Fellowes. Is that clear?"

Miss Fellowes raised her chin. "I understand the orders, Dr. Hoskins, and the nursing profession is accustomed to placing its duties ahead of self-preservation."

"Good. You can always signal if you need anyone." And the two men left.

Miss Fellowes turned to the boy. He was watching her and there was still milk in the saucer. Laboriously, she tried to show him how to lift the saucer and place it to his lips. He resisted, but let her touch him without crying out.

Always, his frightened eyes were on her, watching, watching for the one false move. She found herself soothing him, trying to move her hand very slowly toward his hair, letting him see it every inch of the way, see there was no harm in it.

And she succeeded in stroking his hair for an instant.

She said, "I'm going to have to show you how to use the bathroom. Do you think you can learn?"

She spoke quietly, kindly, knowing he would not understand the words but hoping he would respond to the calmness of the tone.

The boy launched into a clicking phrase again.

She said, "May I take you hand?"

She held out hers and the boy looked at it. She left it outstretched and waited. The boy's own hand crept forward toward hers.

"That's right," she said.

It approached within an inch of hers and then the boy's courage failed him. He snatched it back.

"Well," said Miss Fellowes calmly, "we'll try again later. Would you like to sit down here?" She patted the mattress of the bed.

The hours passed slowly and progress was

minute. She did not succeed either with bath-room or with the bed. In fact, after the child had given unmistakable signs of sleepiness he lay down on the bare ground and then, with a quick movement, rolled beneath the bed.

She bent to look at him and his eyes gleamed out at her as he tongue-clicked at her.

"All right," she said, "if you feel safe there, you sleep there."

She closed the door to the bedroom and re-tired to the cot that had been placed for her use in the largest room. At her insistence, a make-shift canopy had been stretched over it. She thought: Those stupid men will have to place a mirror in this room and a larger chest of draw-ers and a separate washroom if they expect me to spend nights here.

It was difficult to sleep. She found herself straining to hear possible sounds in the next room. He couldn't get out, could he? The walls were sheer and impossibly high but suppose the child could climb like a monkey? Well, Hoskins said there were observational devices watching through the ceiling.

Suddenly she thought: Can he be dangerous? Physically dangerous?

Surely, Hoskins couldn't have meant that. Surely, he would not have left her here alone, if—

She tried to laugh at herself. He was only a three- or four-year-old child. Still, she had not succeeded in cutting his nails. If he should attack her with nails and teeth while she slept——

Her breath came quickly. Oh, ridiculous, and yet——

She listened with painful attentiveness, and this time she heard the sound.

The boy was crying.

Not shrieking in fear or anger; not yelling or screaming. It was crying softly, and the cry was the heartbroken sobbing of a lonely, lonely child.

For the first time, Miss Fellowes thought with a pang: Poor thing!

Of course, it was a child; what did the shape of its head matter? It was a child that had been orphaned as no child had ever been orphaned before. Not only its mother and father were gone, but all its species. Snatched callously out of time, it was now the only creature of its kind in the world. The last. The only.

She felt pity for it strengthen, and with it shame at her own callousness. Tucking her own nightgown carefully about her calves (incongruously, she thought: Tomorrow I'll have to bring in a bathrobe) she got out of bed and went into the boy's room.

"Little boy," she called in a whisper. "Little boy."

She was about to reach under the bed, but she thought of a possible bite and did not. Instead, she turned on the night light and moved the bed.

The poor thing was huddled in the corner, knees up against his chin, looking up at her with blurred and apprehensive eyes.

In the dim light, she was not aware of his repulsiveness.

"Poor boy," she said, "poor boy." She felt him stiffen as she stroked his hair, then relax. "Poor boy. May I hold you?"

She sat down on the floor next to him and slowly and rhythmically stroked his hair, his cheek, his arm. Softly, she began to sing a slow and gentle song.

He lifted his head at that, staring at her mouth in the dimness, as though wondering at the sound.

She maneuvered him closer while he listened to her. Slowly, she pressed gently against the side of his head, until it rested on her shoulder. She put her arm under his thighs and with a smooth and unhurried motion lifted him into her lap.

She continued singing, the same simple verse over and over, while she rocked back and forth, back and forth.

He stopped crying, and after a while the smooth burr of his breathing showed he was asleep.

With infinite care, she pushed his bed back against the wall and laid him down. She covered him and stared down. His face looked so peaceful and little-boy as he slept. It didn't matter so much that it was so ugly. Really.

She began to tiptoe out, then thought: If he wakes up?

She came back, battled irresolutely with herself, then sighed and slowly got into bed with the child.

It was too small for her. She was cramped and uneasy at the lack of canopy, but the child's hand crept into hers and, somehow, she fell asleep in that position.

She awoke with a start and a wild impulse to scream. The latter she just managed to suppress into a gurgle. The boy was looking at her, wide-eyed. It took her a long moment to remember getting into bed with him, and now, slowly, without unfixing her eyes from his, she stretched one leg carefully and let it touch the floor, then the other one.

She cast a quick and apprehensive glance toward the open ceiling, then tensed her muscles for quick disengagement.

But at that moment, the boy's stubby fingers reached out and touched her lips. He said something.

She shrank at the touch. He was terribly ugly in the light of day.

The boy spoke again. He opened his own mouth and gestured with his hand as though something were coming out.

Miss Fellowes guessed at the meaning and said tremulously, "Do you want me to sing?"

The boy said nothing but stared at her mouth.

In a voice slightly off key with tension, Miss Fellowes began the little song she had sung the night before and the ugly little boy smiled. He swayed clumsily in rough time to the music and made a little gurgly sound that might have been the beginnings of a laugh.

Miss Fellowes sighed inwardly. Music hath charms to soothe the savage breast. It might help——

She said, "You wait. Let me get myself fixed

up. It will just take a minute. Then I'll make breakfast for you."

She worked rapidly, conscious of the lack of ceiling at all times. The boy remained in bed, watching her when she was in view. She smiled at him at those times and waved. At the end, he waved back, and she found herself being charmed by that.

Finally, she said, "Would you like oatmeal with milk?" It took a moment to prepare, and then she beckoned to him.

Whether he understood the gesture or followed the aroma, Miss Fellowes did not know, but he got out of bed.

She tried to show him how to use a spoon but he shrank away from it in fright. (Time enough, she thought.) She compromised on insisting that he lift the bowl in his hands. He did it clumsily enough and it was incredibly messy but most of it did get into him.

She tried the drinking milk in a glass this time, and the little boy whined when he found the opening too small for him to get his face into conveniently. She held his hand, forcing it around the glass, making him tip it, forcing his mouth to the rim.

Again a mess but again most went into him, and she was used to messes.

The washroom, to her surprise and relief, was a less frustrating matter. He understood what it was she expected him to do.

She found herself patting his head, saying, "Good boy. Smart boy."

And to Miss Fellowes' exceeding pleasure, the boy smiled at that.

She thought: when he smiles, he's quite bearable. Really.

Later in the day, the gentlemen of the press arrived.

She held the boy in her arms and he clung to her wildly while across the open door they set cameras to work. The commotion frightened the boy and he began to cry, but it was ten minutes before Miss Fellowes was allowed to retreat and put the boy in the next room.

She emerged again, flushed with indignation, walked out of the apartment (for the first time in eighteen hours) and closed the door behind her. "I think you've had enough. It will take me a while to quiet him. Go away."

"Sure, sure," said the gentleman from the *Times-Herald*. "But is that really a Neanderthal or is this some kind of gag?"

"I assure you," said Hoskins' voice, suddenly, from the background, "that this is no gag. The child is authentic Homo neanderthalensis."

"Is it a boy or a girl?"

"Boy," said Miss Fellowes breiefly.

"Ape-boy," said the gentleman from the *News*. "That's what we've got here. Ape-boy. How does he act, Nurse?"

"He acts exactly like a little boy," snapped Miss Fellowes, annoyed into the defensive, "and he is not an ape-boy. His name is—is Timothy, Timmie—and he is perfectly normal in his behavior."

She had chosen the name Timothy at a venture. It was the first that had occurred to her.

"Timmie the Ape-boy," said the gentleman from the *News* and, as it turned out, Timmie the

Ape-boy was the name under which the child became known to the world.

The gentleman from the *Globe* turned to Hoskins and said, "Doc, what do you expect to do with the ape-boy?"

Hoskins shrugged. "My original plan was completed when I proved it possible to bring him here. However, the anthropologists will be very interested, I imagine, and the physiologists. We have here, after all, a creature which is at the edge of being human. We should learn a great deal about ourselves and our ancestry from him."

"How long will you keep him?"

"Until such a time as we need the space more than we need him. Quite a while, perhaps."

The gentleman from the *News* said, "Can you bring it out into the open so we can set up subetheric equipment and put on a real show?"

"I'm sorry, but the child cannot be removed from Stasis."

"Exactly what is Stasis?"

"Ah." Hoskins permitted himself one of his short smiles. "That would take a great deal of explanation, gentlemen. In Stasis, time as we know it doesn't exist. Those rooms are inside an invisible bubble that is not exactly part of our Universe. That is why the child could be plucked out of time as it was."

"Well, wait now," said the gentleman from the *News* discontentedly, "what are you giving us? The nurse goes into the room and out of it."

"And so can any of you," said Hoskins matter-of-factly. "You would be moving parallel to the lines of temporal force and no great energy

gain or loss would be involved. The child, however, was taken from the far past. It moved
across the lines and gained temporal potential.
To move it into the Universe and into our own
time would absorb enough energy to burn out
every line in the place and probably blank out
all power in the city of Washington. We had to
store trash brought with him on the premises
and will have to remove it little by little."

The newsmen were writing down sentences
busily as Hoskins spoke to them. They did not
understand and they were sure their readers
would not, but it sounded scientific and that
was what counted.

The gentleman from the *Times-Herald* said,
"Would you be available for an all-circuit interview tonight?"

"I think so," said Hoskins at once, and they
all moved off.

Miss Fellowes looked after them. She understood all this about Stasis and temporal force
as little as the newsmen but she managed to get
this much. Timmie's imprisonment (she found
herself suddenly thinking of the little boy as
Timmie) was a real one and not one imposed by
the arbitrary fiat of Hoskins. Apparently, it was
impossible to let him out of Stasis at all, ever.

Poor child. Poor child.

She was suddenly aware of his crying and she
hastened in to console him.

Miss Fellowes did not have a chance to see
Hoskins on the all-circuit hookup, and though
his interview was beamed to every part of the
world and even to the outpost on the Moon, it

did not penetrate the apartment in which Miss Fellowes and the ugly little boy lived.

But he was down the next morning, radiant and joyful.

Miss Fellowes said, "Did the interview go well?"

"Extremely. And how is—Timmie?"

Miss Fellowes found herself pleased at the use of the name. "Doing quite well. Now come out here, Timmie, the nice gentleman will not hurt you."

But Timmie stayed in the other room, with a lock of his matted hair showing behind the barrier of the door and, occasionally, the corner of an eye.

"Actually," said Miss Fellowes, "he is settling down amazingly. He is quite intelligent."

"Are you surprised?"

She hesitated just a moment, then said, "Yes, I am. I suppose I thought he was an ape-boy."

"Well, ape-boy or not, he's done a great deal for us. He's put Stasis, Inc. on the map. We're in, Miss Fellowes, we're in." It was as though he had to express his triumph to someone, even if only to Miss Fellowes.

"Oh?" She let him talk.

He put his hands in his pockets and said, "We've been working on a shoestring for ten years, scrounging funds a penny at a time wherever we could. We had to shoot the works on one big show. It was everything, or nothing. And when I say the works, I mean it. This attempt to bring in a Neanderthal took every cent we could borrow or steal, and some of it *was* stolen—funds for other projects, used for this one without permission. If that experiment hadn't succeeded, I'd have been through."

Miss Fellowes said abruptly, "Is that why there are no ceilings?"

"Eh?" Hoskins looked up.

"Was there no money for ceilings?"

"Oh. Well, that wasn't the only reason. We didn't really know in advance how old the Neanderthal might be exactly. We can detect only dimly in time, and he might have been large and savage. It was possible we might have had to deal with him from a distance, like a caged animal."

"But since that hasn't turned out to be so, I suppose you can build a ceiling now."

"Now, yes. We have plenty of money, now. Funds have been promised from every source. This is all wonderful, Miss Fellowes." His broad face gleamed with a smile that lasted and when he left, even his back seemed to be smiling.

Miss Fellowes thought: He's quite a nice man when he's off guard and forgets about being scientific.

She wondered for an idle moment if he was married, then dismissed the thought in self-embarrassment.

"Timmie," she called. "Come here, Timmie."

In the months that passed, Miss Fellowes felt herself grow to be an integral part of Stasis, Inc. She was given a small office of her own with her name on the door, an office quite close to the dollhouse (as she never stopped calling Timmie's Stasis bubble). She was given a substantial raise. The dollhouse was covered by a ceiling; its furnishings were elaborated and improved; a second washroom was added—and even so, she gained an apartment of her own on the institute grounds and, on occasion, did not stay with Timmie during the night. An intercom was set up between the dollhouse and her apartment and Timmie learned how to use it.

Miss Fellowes got used to Timmie. She even grew less conscious of his ugliness. One day she found herself staring at an ordinary boy in the street and finding something bulgy and unattractive in his high domed forehead and jutting chin. She had to shake herself to break the spell.

It was more pleasant to grow used to Hoskins' occasional visits. It was obvious he welcomed escape from his increasingly harried role as head of Stasis, Inc., and that he took a sentimental interest in the child who had started it all, but it seemed to Miss Fellowes that he also enjoyed talking to her.

(She had learned some facts about Hoskins, too. He had invented the method of analyzing the reflection of the past-penetrating mesonic beam; he had invented the method of establishing Stasis; his coldness was only an effort to hide a kindly nature; and, oh yes, he *was* married.)

What Miss Fellowes could *not* get used to was the fact that she was engaged in a scientific experiment. Despite all she could do, she found herself getting personally involved to the point of quarreling with the physiologists.

On one occasion, Hoskins came down and found her in the midst of a hot urge to kill. They had no right; they had no *right*—— Even if he *was* a Neanderthal, he still wasn't an animal.

She was staring after them in a blind fury; staring out the open door and listening to Timmie's sobbing, when she noticed Hoskins standing before her. He might have been there for minutes.

He said, "May I come in?"

She nodded curtly, then hurried to Timmie, who clung to her, curling his little bandy legs—still thin, so thin—about her.

Hoskins watched, then said gravely, "He seems quite unhappy."

Miss Fellowes said, "I don't blame him. They're at him every day now with their blood samples and their probings. They keep him on synthetic diets that I wouldn't feed a pig."

"It's the sort of thing they can't try on a human, you know."

"And they can't try it on Timmie, either. Dr. Hoskins, I insist. You told me it was Timmie's coming that put Stasis, Inc. on the map. If you have any gratitude for that at all, you've *got* to keep them away from the poor thing at least until he's old enough to understand a little more. After he's had a bad session with them, he has nightmares, he can't sleep. Now I warn you," (she reached a sudden peak of fury) "I'm not letting them in here any more."

(She realized that she had screamed that, but she couldn't help it.)

She said more quietly, "I know he's Neanderthal but there's a great deal we don't appreciate about Neanderthals. I've read up on them. They had a culture of their own. Some of the greatest human inventions arose in Neanderthal times. The domestication of animals, for instance; the wheel; various techniques in grinding stone. They even had spiritual yearnings. They buried their dead and buried possessions with the body, showing they believed in a life after death. It amounts to the fact that they invented religion. Doesn't that mean Timmie has a right to human treatment?"

She patted the little boy gently on his buttocks and sent him off into his playroom. As the door was opened, Hoskins smiled briefly at the display of toys that could be seen.

Miss Fellowes said defensively, "The poor child deserves his toys. It's all he has and he earns them with what he goes through."

"No, no. No objections, I assure you. I was just thinking how you've changed since the first day, when you were quite angry I had foisted a Neanderthal on you."

Miss Fellowes said in a low voice, "I suppose I didn't——" and faded off.

Hoskins changed the subject, "How old would you say he is, Miss Fellowes?"

She said, "I can't say, since we don't know how Neanderthals develop. In size, he'd only be three but Neanderthals are smaller generally and with all the tampering they do with him, he probably isn't growing. The way he's learning English, though, I'd say he was well over four."

"Really? I haven't noticed anything about learning English in the reports."

"He won't speak to anyone but me. For now, anyway. He's terribly afraid of others, and no wonder. But he can ask for an article of food;

he can indicate any need practically; and he understands almost anything I say. Of course," (she watched him shrewdly, trying to estimate if this was the time), "his development may not continue."

"Why not?"

"Any child needs stimulation and this one lives a life of solitary confinement. I do what I can, but I'm not with him all the time and I'm not all he needs. What I mean, Dr. Hoskins, is that he needs another boy to play with."

Hoskins nodded slowly. "Unfortunately, there's only one of him, isn't there? Poor child."

Miss Fellowes warmed to him at once. She said, "You do like Timmie, don't you?" It was so nice to have someone else feel like that.

"Oh, yes," said Hoskins, and with his guard down, she could see the weariness in his eyes.

Miss Fellowes dropped her plans to push the matter at once. She said, with real concern, "You look worn out, Dr. Hoskins."

"Do I, Miss Fellowes? I'll have to practice looking more lifelike then."

"I suppose Stasis, Inc. is very busy and that that keeps you very busy."

Hoskins shrugged. "You suppose right. It's a matter of animal, vegetable, and mineral in equal parts, Miss Fellowes. But then, I suppose you haven't ever seen our displays."

"Actually, I haven't. ——But it's not because I'm not interested. It's just that I've been so busy."

"Well, you're not all that busy right now," he said with impulsive decision. "I'll call for you tomorrow at eleven and give you a personal tour. How's that?"

She smiled happily. "I'd love it."

He nodded and smiled in his turn and left.

Miss Fellowes hummed at intervals for the rest of the day. Really—to think so was ridiculous, of course—but really, it was almost like—like making a date.

He was quite on time the next day, smiling and pleasant. She had replaced her nurse's uniform with a dress. One of conservative cut, to be sure, but she hadn't felt so feminine in years.

He complimented her on her appearance with staid formality and she accepted with equally formal grace. It was really a perfect prelude, she thought. And then the additional thought came, prelude to what?

She shut that off by hastening to say good-by to Timmie and to assure him she would be back soon. She made sure he knew all about what and where lunch was.

Hoskins took her into the new wing, into which she had never yet gone. It still had the odor of newness about it and the sound of construction, softly heard, was indication enough that it was still being extended.

"Animal, vegetable, and mineral," said Hoskins, as he had the day before. "Animal right there; our most spectacular exhibits."

The space was divided into many rooms, each a separate Stasis bubble. Hoskins brought her to the view-glass of one and she looked in. What she saw impressed her first as a scaled, tailed chicken. Skittering on two thin legs it ran from wall to wall with its delicate birdlike head, surmounted by a bony keel like the comb of a rooster, looking this way and that. The paws on its small forelimbs clenched and unclenched constantly.

Hoskins said, "It's our dinosaur. We've had it for months. I don't know when we'll be able to let go of it."

"Dinosaur?"

"Did you expect a giant?"

She dimpled. "One does, I suppose. I know some of them are small."

"A small one is all we aimed for, believe me. Generally, it's under investigation, but this seems to be an open hour. Some interesting things have been discovered. For instance, it is not entirely cold-blooded. It has an imperfect method of maintaining internal temperatures higher than that of its environment. Unfortunately, it's a male. Ever since we brought it in we've been trying to get a fix on another that may be female, but we've had no luck yet."

"Why female?"

He looked at her quizzically. "So that we might have a fighting chance to obtain fertile eggs, and baby dinosaurs."

"Of course."

He led her to the trilobite section. "That's Professor Dwayne of Washington University," he said. "He's a nuclear chemist. If I recall correctly, he's taking an isotope ratio on the oxygen of the water."

"Why?"

"It's primeval water; at least half a billion years old. The isotope ratio gives the temperature of the ocean at that time. He himself happens to ignore the trilobites, but others are chiefly concerned in dissecting them. They're the lucky ones because all they need are scalpels and microscopes. Dwayne has to set up a mass spectrograph each time he conducts an experiment."

"Why's that? Can't he——"

"No, he can't. He can't take anything out of the room as far as can be helped."

There were samples of primordial plant life too and chunks of rock formations. Those were the vegetable and mineral. And every specimen had its investigator. It was like a museum; a museum brought to life and serving as a superactive center of research.

"And you have to supervise all of this, Dr. Hoskins?"

"Only indirectly, Miss Fellowes. I have subordinates, thank heaven. My own interest is entirely in the theoretical aspects of the matter: the nature of Time, the technique of mesonic intertemporal detection and so on. I would exchange all this for a method of detecting objects closer in Time than ten thousand years ago. If we could get into historical times——"

He was interrupted by a commotion at one of the distant booths, a thin voice raised querulously. He frowned, muttered hastily, "Excuse me," and hastened off.

Miss Fellowes followed as best she could without actually running.

An elderly man, thinly-bearded and red-faced, was saying, "I had vital aspects of my investigations to complete. Don't you understand that?"

A uniformed technician with the interwoven SI monogram (for Stasis, Inc.) on his lab coat, said, "Dr. Hoskins, it was arranged with Professor Ademewski at the beginning that the specimen could only remain here two weeks."

I did not know then how long my investigations would take. I'm not a prophet," said Ademewski heatedly.

Dr. Hoskins said, "You understand, Professor, we have limited space; we must keep specimens rotating. That piece of chalcopyrite must go back; there are men waiting for the next specimen."

"Why can't I have it for myself, then? Let me take it out of there."

"You know you can't have it."

"A piece of chalcopyrite; a miserable five-kilogram piece? Why not?"

"We can't afford the energy expense!" said Hoskins brusquely. "You know that."

The technician interrupted. "The point is, Dr. Hoskins, that he tried to remove the rock against the rules and I almost punctured Stasis while he was in there, not knowing he was in there."

There was a short silence and Dr. Hoskins turned on the investigator with a cold formality, "Is that so, Professor?"

Professor Ademewski coughed, "I saw no harm—"

Hoskins reached up to a hand-pull dangling just within reach, outside the specimen room in question. He pulled it.

Miss Fellowes, who had been peering in, looking at the totally undistinguished sample of rock that occasioned the dispute, drew in her breath sharply as its existence flickered out. The room was empty.

Hoskins said, "Professor, your permit to investigate matters in Stasis will be permanently voided. I am sorry."

"But wait——"

"I am sorry. You have violated one of the stringent rules."

"I will appeal to the International Association—"

"Appeal away. In a case like this, you will find I can't be overruled."

He turned away deliberately, leaving the professor still protesting and said to Miss Fellowes (his face still white with anger), "Would you care to have lunch with me, Miss Fellowes?"

He took her into the small administration alcove of the cafeteria. He greeted others and introduced Miss Fellowes with complete ease, although she herself felt painfully self-conscious.

What must they think, she thought, and tried desperately to appear businesslike.

She said, "Do you have that kind of trouble often, Dr. Hoskins? I mean like that you just had with the professor?" She took her fork in hand and began eating.

"No," said Hoskins forcefully. "That was the first time. Of course I'm always having to argue men out of removing specimens but this is the first time one actually tried to *do* it."

"I remember you once talked about the energy it would consume."

"That's right. Of course, we've tried to take it into account. Accidents will happen and so we've got special power sources designed to stand the drain of accidental removal from Stasis, but that doesn't mean we want to see a year's supply of energy gone in half a second— or can afford to without having our plans of expansion delayed for years. ——Besides, imagine the professor's being in the room while Stasis was about to be punctured."

"What would have happened to him if it had been?"

"Well, we've experimented with inanimate objects and with mice and they've disappeared. Presumably they've traveled back in time; carried along, so to speak, by the pull of the object simultaneously snapping back into its natural time. For that reason, we have to anchor objects within Stasis that we don't want to move and that's a complicated procedure. The professor would not have been anchored and he would have gone back to the Pliocene at the moment when we abstracted the rock—plus, of course, the two weeks it had remained here in the present."

"How dreadful it would have been."

"Not on account of the professor, I assure you. If he were fool enough to do what he did, it would serve him right. But imagine the effect it would have on the public if the fact came out. All people would need is to become aware of the dangers involved and funds could be choked off like that." He snapped his fingers and played moodily with his food.

Miss Fellowes said, "Couldn't you get him back? The way you got the rock in the first place?"

"No, because once an object is returned, the original fix is lost unless we deliberately plan to retain it and there was no reason to do that in this case. There never is. Finding the professor again would mean relocating a specific fix and that would be like dropping a line into the oceanic abyss for the purpose of dredging up a particular fish. ——My God, when I think of the precautions we take to prevent accidents, it makes me mad. We have every individual Stasis unit set up with its own puncturing device—we have to, since each unit has its separate fix and must be collapsible independently. The point is, though, none of the puncturing devices is ever activated until the last minute. And then we deliberately make activation impossible except by the pull of a rope carefully led outside the Stasis. The pull is a gross mechanical motion that requires a strong effort, not something that is likely to be done accidentally."

Miss Fellowes said, "But doesn't it—change history to move something in and out of Time?"

Hoskins shrugged. "Theoretically, yes; actually, except in unusual cases, no. We move objects out of Stasis all the time. Air molecules. Bacteria. Dust. About 10 percent of our energy consumption goes to make up micro-losses of that nature. But moving even large objects in Time sets up changes that damp out. Take that chalcopyrite from the Pliocene. Because of its

absence for two weeks some insect didn't find
the shelter it might have found and is killed.
That could initiate a whole series of changes,
but the mathematics of Stasis indicates that this
is a converging series. The amount of change
diminishes with time and then things are as before."

"You mean, reality heals itself?"

"In a manner of speaking. Abstract a human
from time or send one back, and you make a
larger wound. If the individual is an ordinary
one, that wound still heals itself. Of course,
there are a great many people who write to us
each day and want us to bring Abraham Lincoln
into the present, or Mohammed, or Lenin. *That*
can't be done, of course. Even if we could find
them, the change in reality in moving one of the
history molders would be too great to be healed.
There are ways of calculating when a change is
likely to be too great and we avoid even approaching that limit."

Miss Fellowes said, "Then, Timmie—"

"No, he presents no problem in that direction. Reality is safe. But——" He gave her a
quick, sharp glance, then went on, "But never
mind. Yesterday you said Timmie needed companionship."

"Yes," Miss Fellowes smiled her delight. "I
didn't think you paid that any attention."

"Of course I did. I'm fond of the child. I appreciate your feelings for him and I was concerned enough to want to explain to you. Now
I have; you've seen what we do; you've gotten
some insight into the difficulties involved; so

you know why, with the best will in the world, we can't supply companionship for Timmie."

"You can't?" said Miss Fellowes, with sudden dismay.

"But I've just explained. We couldn't possibly expect to find another Neanderthal his age without incredible luck, and if we could, it wouldn't be fair to multiply risks by having another human being in Stasis."

Miss Fellowes put down her spoon and said energetically, "But, Dr. Hoskins, that is not at all what I meant. I don't want you to bring another Neanderthal into the present. I know that's impossible. But it isn't impossible to bring another child to play with Timmie."

Hoskins stared at her in concern. "A *human* child?"

"*Another* child," said Miss Fellowes, completely hostile now. "Timmie is human."

"I couldn't dream of such a thing."

"Why not? Why couldn't you? What is wrong with the notion? You pulled that child out of Time and made him an eternal prisoner. Don't you owe him something? Dr. Hoskins, if there is any man who, in this world, is that child's father in every sense but the biological, it is you. Why can't you do this little thing for him?"

Hoskins said, "His *father*?" He rose, somewhat unsteadily, to his feet. "Miss Fellowes, I think I'll take you back now, if you don't mind."

They returned to the dollhouse in a complete silence that neither broke.

It was a long time after that before she saw Hoskins again, except for an occasional glimpse in passing. She was sorry about that at times; then, at other times, when Timmie was more than usually woebegone or when he spent silent hours at the window with its prospect of little more than nothing, she thought, fiercely: Stupid man.

Timmie's speech grew better and more precise each day. It never entirely lost a certain soft, slurriness that Miss Fellowes found rather endearing. In times of excitement, he fell back into tongue-clicking but those times were becoming fewer. He must be forgetting the days before he came into the present—except for dreams.

As he grew older, the physiologists grew less interested and the psychologists more so. Miss Fellowes was not sure that she did not like the new group even less than the first. The needles were gone; the injections and withdrawals of fluid; the special diets. But now Timmie was made to overcome barriers to reach food and water. He had to lift panels, move bars, reach for cords. And the mild electric shocks made him cry and drove Miss Fellowes to distraction.

She did not wish to appeal to Hoskins; she did not wish to have to go to him; for each time she thought of him, she thought of his face over the luncheon table that last time. Her eyes moistened and she thought: Stupid, *stupid* man.

And then one day Hoskins' voice sounded unexpectedly, calling into the dollhouse, "Miss Fellowes."

She came out coldly, smoothing her nurse's uniform, then stopped in confusion at finding herself in the presence of a pale woman, slender and of middle height. The woman's fair hair and complexion gave her an appearance of fragility. Standing behind her and clutching at her skirt was a round-faced, large-eyed child of four.

Hoskins said, "Dear, this is Miss Fellowes, the nurse in charge of the boy. Miss Fellowes, this is my wife."

(Was this his wife? She was not as Miss Fellowes had imagined her to be. But then, why not? A man like Hoskins would choose a weak thing to be his foil. If that was what he wanted——)

She forced a matter-of-fact greeting. "Good afternoon, Mrs. Hoskins. Is this your—your little boy?"

(*That* was a surprise. She had thought of Hoskins as a husband, but not as a father, except, of course—— She suddenly caught Hoskins' grave eyes and flushed.)

Hoskins said, "Yes, this is my boy, Jerry. Say hello to Miss Fellowes, Jerry."

(Had he stressed the word "this" just a bit? Was he saying *this* was his son and not——)

Jerry receded a bit further into the folds of the maternal skirt and muttered his hello. Mrs. Hoskins' eyes were searching over Miss Fellowes' shoulders, peering into the room, looking for something.

Hoskins said, "Well, let's go in. Come, dear. There's a trifling discomfort at the threshold, but it passes."

Miss Fellowes said, "Do you want Jerry to come in, too?"

"Of course. He is to be Timmie's playmate.

You said that Timmie needed a playmate. Or have you forgotten?"

"But——" She looked at him with a colossal, surprised wonder. "*Your* boy?"

He said peevishly, "Well, whose boy, then? Isn't this what you want? Come on in, dear. Come on in."

Mrs. Hoskins lifted Jerry into her arms with a distinct effort and, hesitantly, stepped over the threshold. Jerry squirmed as she did so, disliking the sensation.

Mrs. Hoskins said in a thin voice, "Is the creature here? I don't see him."

Miss Fellowes called, "Timmie. Come out."

Timmie peered around the edge of the door, staring up at the little boy who was visiting him. The muscles in Mrs. Hoskins' arms tensed visibly.

She said to her husband, "Gerald, are you sure it's safe?"

Miss Fellowes said at once, "If you mean is Timmie safe, why, of course he is. He's a gentle little boy."

"But he's a sa—savage."

(The ape-boy stories in the newspapers!) Miss Fellowes said emphatically, "He's not a savage. He is just as quiet and reasonable as you can possibly expect a five-and-a-half-year-old to be. It is very generous of you, Mrs. Hoskins, to agree to allow your boy to play with Timmie but please have no fears about it."

Mrs. Hoskins said with mild heat, "I'm not sure that I agree."

"We've had it out, dear," said Hoskins. "Let's

not bring up the matter for new argument. Put Jerry down.".

Mrs. Hoskins did so and the boy backed against her, staring at the pair of eyes which were staring back at him from the next room.

"Come here, Timmie," said Miss Fellowes. "Don't be afraid."

Slowly, Timmie stepped into the room. Hoskins bent to disengage Jerry's fingers from his mother's skirt. "Step back, dear. Give the children a chance."

The youngsters faced one another. Although the younger, Jerry was nevertheless an inch taller, and in the presence of his straightness and his high-held, well-proportioned head, Timmie's grotesqueries were suddenly almost as pronounced as they had been in the first days.

Miss Fellowes' lips quivered.

It was the little Neanderthal who spoke first, in childish treble. "What's your name?" And Timmie thrust his face suddenly forward as though to inspect the other's features more closely.

Startled Jerry responded with a vigorous shove that sent Timmie tumbling. Both began crying loudly and Mrs. Hoskins snatched up her child, while Miss Fellowes, flushed with repressed anger, lifted Timmie and comforted him.

Mrs. Hoskins said, "They just instinctively don't like one another."

"No more instinctively," said her husband wearily, "than any two children dislike each other. Now put Jerry down and let him get used to the situation. In fact, we had better leave.

Miss Fellowes can bring Jerry to my office after a while and I'll have him taken home."

The two children spent the next hour very aware of each other. Jerry cried for his mother, struck out at Miss Fellowes and, finally, allowed himself to be comforted with a lollipop. Timmie sucked at another, and at the end of an hour, Miss Fellowes had them playing with the same set of blocks, though at opposite ends of the room.

She found herself almost maudlinly grateful to Hoskins when she brought Jerry to him.

She searched for ways to thank him but his very formality was a rebuff. Perhaps he could not forgive her for making him feel like a cruel father. Perhaps the bringing of his own child was an attempt, after all, to prove himself both a kind father to Timmie and, also, not his father at all. Both at the same time!

So all she could say was, "Thank you. Thank you very much."

And all he could say was, "It's all right. Don't mention it."

It became a settled routine. Twice a week, Jerry was brought in for an hour's play, later extended to two hours' play. The children learned each other's names and ways and played together.

And yet, after the first rush of gratitude, Miss Fellowes found herself disliking Jerry. He was larger and heavier and in all things dominant, forcing Timmie into a completely secondary role. All that reconciled her to the situation was the fact that, despite difficulties, Timmie looked forward with more and more delight to the periodic appearances of his playfellow.

It was all he had, she mourned to herself.

And once, as she watched them, she thought: Hoskins' two children, one by his wife and one by Stasis.

While she herself——

Heavens, she thought, putting her fists to her temples and feeling ashamed: I'm jealous!

"Miss Fellowes," said Timmie (carefully, she had never allowed him to call her anything else) "when will I go to school?"

She looked down at those eager brown eyes turned up to hers and passed her hand softly through his thick, curly hair. It was the most disheveled portion of his appearance, for she cut his hair herself while he sat restlessly under the scissors. She did not ask for professional help, for the very clumsiness of the cut served to mask the retreating fore part of the skull and the bulging hinder part.

She said, "Where did you hear about school?"

"Jerry goes to school. Kin-der-gar-ten." He said it carefully. "There arc lots of places he goes. Outside. When can I go outside, Miss Fellowes?"

A small pain centered in Miss Fellowes' heart. Of course, she saw, there would be no way of avoiding the inevitability of Timmie's hearing more and more of the outer world he could never enter.

She said, with an attempt at gaiety, "Why, whatever would you do in kindergarten, Timmie?"

"Jerry says they play games, they have picture tapes. He says there are lots of children.

He says—he says——" A thought, then a tri-
umphant upholding of both small hands with
the fingers splayed apart. "He says this many."

Miss Fellowes said, "Would you like picture
tapes? I can get you picture tapes. Very nice
ones. And music tapes too."

So that Timmie was temporarily comforted.

He pored over the picture tapes in Jerry's
absence and Miss Fellowes read to him out of
ordinary books by the hours.

There was so much to explain in even the sim-
plest story, so much that was outside the per-
spective of his three rooms. Timmie took to
having his dreams more often now that the outside was being introduced to him.

They were always the same, about the outside. He tried haltingly to describe them to Miss
Fellowes. In his dreams, he was outside, an
empty outside, but very large, with children and
queer indescribable objects half-digested in his
thought out of bookish descriptions half-
understood, or out of distant Neanderthal
memories half-recalled.

But the children and objects ignored him and
though he was in the world, he was never part
of it, but was as alone as though he were in his
own room—and would wake up crying.

Miss Fellowes tried to laugh at the dreams,
but there were nights in her own apartment
when she cried, too.

One day, as Miss Fellowes read, Timmie put
his hand under her chin and lifted it gently so
that her eyes left the book and met his.

He said, "How do you know what to say, Miss Fellowes?"

She said, "You see these marks? They tell me what to say. These marks make words."

He stared at them long and curiously, taking the book out of her hands. "Some of these marks are the same."

She laughed with pleasure at this sign of his shrewdness and said, "So they are. Would you like to have me show you how to make the marks?"

"All right. That would be a nice game."

It did not occur to her that he could learn to read. Up to the very moment that he read a book to her, it did not occur to her that he could learn to read.

Then, weeks later, the enormity of what had been done struck her. Timmie sat in her lap, following word by word the printing in a child's book, reading to her. He was reading to her!

She struggled to her feet in amazement and said, "Now Timmie, I'll be back later. I want to see Dr. Hoskins."

Excited nearly to frenzy, it seemed to her she might have an answer to Timmie's unhappiness. If Timmie could not leave to enter the world, the world must be brought into those three rooms to Timmie—the whole world in books and film and sound. He must be educated to his full capacity. So much the world owed him.

She found Hoskins in a mood that was oddly analogous to her own; a kind of triumph and glory. His offices were unusually busy, and for a moment, she thought she would not get to see him, as she stood abashed in the anteroom.

But he saw her, and a smile spread over his broad face. "Miss Fellowes, come here."

He spoke rapidly into the intercom, then shut it off. "Have you heard? ——No, of course, you couldn't have. We've done it. We've actually done it. We have intertemporal detection at close range."

"You mean," she tried to detach her thought from her own good news for a moment, "that you can get a person from historical times into the present?"

"That's just what I mean. We have a fix on a fourteenth century individual right now. Imagine. *Imagine!* If you could only know how glad I'll be to shift from the eternal concentration on the Mesozoic, replace the paleontologists with the historians—— But there's something you wish to say to me, eh? Well, go ahead; go ahead. You find me in a good mood. Anything you want you can have."

Miss Fellowes smiled. "I'm glad. Because I wonder if we might not establish a system of instruction for Timmie?"

"Instruction? In what?"

"Well, in everything. A school. So that he might learn."

"But *can* he learn?"

"Certainly, he *is* learning. He can read. I've taught him so much myself."

Hoskins sat there, seeming suddenly depressed. "I don't know, Miss Fellowes."

She said, "You just said that anything I wanted—"

"I know and I should not have. You see, Miss Fellowes, I'm sure you must realize that we cannot maintain the Timmie experiment forever."

She stared at him with sudden horror, not really understanding what he had said. How did he mean "cannot maintain"? With an agonizing flash of recollection, she recalled Professor Ademewski and his mineral specimen that was taken away after two weeks. She said, "But you're talking about a boy. Not about a rock—"

Dr. Hoskins said uneasily, "Even a boy can't be given undue importance, Miss Fellowes. Now that we expect individuals out of historical time, we will need Stasis space, all we can get."

She didn't grasp it. "But you can't. Timmie—Timmie—"

"Now, Miss Fellowes, please don't upset yourself. Timmie won't go right away; perhaps not for months. Meanwhile we'll do what we can."

She was still staring at him.

"Let me get you something, Miss Fellowes."

"No," she whispered. "I don't need anything." She arose in a kind of nightmare and left.

Timmie, she thought, you will *not* die. You will *not* die.

It was all very well to hold tensely to the thought that Timmie must not die, but how was that to be arranged? In the first weeks, Miss

Fellowes clung only to the hope that the attempt to bring forward a man from the fourteenth century would fail completely. Hoskins' theories might be wrong or his practice defective. Then things could go on as before.

Certainly, that was not the hope of the rest of the world and, irrationally, Miss Fellowes hated the world for it. "Project Middle Ages" reached a climax of white-hot publicity. The press and the public had hungered for something like this. Stasis, Inc. had lacked the necessary sensation for a long time now. A new rock or another ancient fish failed to stir them. But *this* was *it*.

A historical human; an adult speaking a known language; someone who could open a new page of history to the scholar.

Zero-time was coming and this time it was not a question of three onlookers from the balcony. This time there would be a world-wide audience. This time the technicians of Stasis, Inc. would play their role before nearly all of mankind.

Miss Fellowes was herself all but savage with waiting. When young Jerry Hoskins showed up for his scheduled playtime with Timmie, she scarcely recognized him. He was not the one she was waiting for.

(The secretary who brought him left hurriedly after the barest nod for Miss Fellowes. She was rushing for a good place from which to watch the climax of Project Middle Ages. ——And so ought Miss Fellowes with far better reason, she thought bitterly, if only that stupid girl would arrive.)

Jerry Hoskins sidled toward her, embarrassed. "Miss Fellowes?" He took the reproduction of a news-strip out of his pocket.

"Yes? What is it, Jerry?"

"Is this a picture of Timmie?"

Miss Fellowes stared at him, then snatched the strip from Jerry's hand. The excitement of Project Middle Ages had brought about a pale revival of interest in Timmie on the part of the presss.

Jerry watched her narrowly, then said, "It says Timmie is an ape-boy. What does that mean?"

Miss Fellowes caught the youngster's wrist and repressed the impulse to shake him. "Never say that, Jerry. Never, do you understand? It is a nasty word and you mustn't use it."

Jerry struggled out of her grip, frightened.

Miss Fellowes tore up the news-strip with a vicious twist of the wrist. "Now go inside and play with Timmie. He's got a new book to show you."

And then, finally, the girl appeared. Miss Fellowes did not know her. None of the usual stand-ins she had used when business took her elsewhere was available now, not with Project Middle Ages at climax, but Hoskins' secretary had promised to find *someone* and this must be the girl.

Miss Fellowes tried to keep querulousness out of her voice. "Are you the girl assigned to Stasis Section One?"

"Yes, I'm Mandy Terris. You're Miss Fellowes, aren't you?"

"That's right."

"I'm sorry I'm late. There's just so much excitement."

"I know. Now I want you——"

Mandy said, "You'll be watching, I suppose." Her thin, vacuously pretty face filled with envy.

"Never mind that. Now I want you to come inside and meet Timmie and Jerry. They will be playing for the next two hours so they'll be giving you no trouble. They've got milk handy and plenty of toys. In fact, it will be better if you leave them alone as much as possible. Now I'll show you where everything is located and——"

"Is it Timmie that's the ape-b——"

"Timmie is the Stasis subject," said Miss Fellowes firmly.

"I mean, he's the one who's not supposed to get out, is that right?"

"Yes. Now, come in. There isn't much time."

And when she finally left, Mandy Terris called after her shrilly, "I hope you get a good seat and, golly, I sure hope it works."

Miss Fellowes did not trust herself to make a reasonable response. She hurried on without looking back.

But the delay meant she did *not* get a good seat. She got no nearer than the wall-viewing-plate in the assembly hall. Bitterly, she regretted that. If she could have been on the spot; if she could somehow have reached out for some sensitive portion of the instrumentations; if she were in some way able to wreck the experiment—

She found the strength to beat down her madness. Simple destruction would have done no good. They would have rebuilt and reconstructed and made the effort again. And she would never be allowed to return to Timmie.

Nothing would help. Nothing but that the experiment itself fail; that it break down irretrievably.

So she waited through the countdown, watching every move on the giant screen, scanning the faces of the technicians as the focus shifted from one to the other, watching for the look of worry and uncertainty that would mark something going unexpectedly wrong; watching, watching——

There was no such look. The count reached zero, and very quietly, very unassumingly, the experiment succeeded!

In the new Stasis that had been established there stood a bearded, stoop-shouldered peasant of indeterminate age, in ragged dirty clothing and wooden shoes, staring in dull horror at the sudden mad change that had flung itself over him.

And while the world went mad with jubilation, Miss Fellowes stood frozen in sorrow, jostled and pushed, all but trampled; surrounded by triumph while bowed down with defeat.

And when the loud-speaker called her name with strident force, it sounded it three times before she responded.

"Miss Fellowes. Miss Fellowes. You are wanted in Stasis Section One immediately. Miss Fellowes. Miss Fell——"

"Let me through!" she cried breathlessly, while the loud-speaker continued its repetitions without pause. She forced her way through the crowds with wild energy, beating at it, striking out with closed fists, flailing, moving toward the door in a nightmare slowness.

Mandy Terris was in tears. "I don't know how it happened. I just went down to the edge of the corridor to watch a pocket-viewing-plate they had put up. Just for a minute. And then before I could move or do anything——" She cried out in sudden accusation, "You said they would make no trouble; you *said* to leave them alone——"

Miss Fellowes, disheveled and trembling uncontrollably, glared at her. "Where's Timmie?"

A nurse was swabbing the arm of a wailing Jerry with disinfectant and another was preparing an anti-tetanus shot. There was blood on Jerry's clothes.

"He bit me, Miss Fellowes," Jerry cried in rage. "He *bit* me."

But Miss Fellowes didn't even see him.

"What did you do with Timmie?" she cried out.

"I locked him in the bathroom," said Mandy. "I just threw the little monster in there and locked him in."

Miss Fellowes ran into the dollhouse. She fumbled at the bathroom door. It took an eternity to get it open and to find the ugly little boy cowering in the corner.

"Don't whip me, Miss Fellowes," he whispered. His eyes were red. His lips were quivering. "I didn't mean to do it."

"Oh, Timmie, who told you about whips?" She caught him to her, hugging him wildly.

He said tremulously, "She said, with a long rope. She said you would hit me and hit me."

"You won't be. She was wicked to say so. But what happened? What happened?"

"He called me an ape-boy. He said I wasn't a real boy. He said I was an animal." Timmie dissolved in a flood of tears. "He said he wasn't going to play with a monkey anymore. I said I wasn't a monkey; I *wasn't* a monkey. He said I was all funny-looking. He said I was horrible ugly. He kept saying and saying and I bit him."

They were both crying now. Miss Fellowes sobbed, "But it isn't true. You know that, Timmie. You're a real boy. You're a dear real boy and the best boy in the world. And no one, *no* one will ever take you away from me."

It was easy to make up her mind, now; easy to know what to do. Only it had to be done quickly. Hoskins wouldn't wait much longer, with his own son mangled——

No, it would have to be done this night, *this* night; with the place four-fifths asleep and the remaining fifth intellectually drunk over Project Middle Ages.

It would be an unusual time for her to return but not an unheard of one. The guard knew her well and would not dream of questioning her. He would think nothing of her carrying a suitcase. She rehearsed the noncommittal phrase, "Games for the boy," and the calm smile.

Why shouldn't he believe that?

He did. When she entered the dollhouse again, Timmie was still awake, and she maintained a desperate normality to avoid frightening him. She talked about his dreams with him and listened to him ask wistfully after Jerry.

There would be few to see her afterward, none to question the bundle she would be carrying. Timmie would be very quiet and then it would be a *fait accompli.* It would be done and what would be the use of trying to undo it. They would leave her be. They would leave them both be.

She opened the suitcases, took out the overcoat, the woolen cap with the ear-flaps and the rest.

Timmie said, with the beginning of alarm, "Why are you putting all these clothes on me, Miss Fellowes?"

She said, "I am going to take you outside, Timmie. To where your dreams are."

"My dreams?" His face twisted in sudden yearning, yet fear was there, too.

"You won't be afraid. You'll be with me. You won't be afraid if you're with me, will you, Timmie?"

"No, Miss Fellowes." He buried his little mis-shapen head against her side, and under her enclosing arm she could feel his small heart thud.

It was midnight and she lifted him into her arms. She disconnected the alarm and opened the door softly.

And she screamed, for facing her across the open door was Hoskins!

There were two men with him and he stared at her, as astonished as she.

Miss Fellowes recovered first by a second and made a quick attempt to push past him; but even with the second's delay he had time. He caught her roughly and hurled her back against a chest of drawers. He waved the men in and confronted her, blocking the door.

"I didn't expect this. Are you completely insane?"

She had managed to interpose her shoulder so that it, rather than Timmie, had struck the chest. She said pleadingly, "What harm can it do if I take him, Dr. Hoskins? You can't put energy loss ahead of a human life?"

Firmly, Hoskins took Timmie out of her arms. "An energy loss this size would mean millions of dollars lost out of the pockets of investors. It would mean a terrible setback for Stasis, Inc. It would mean eventual publicity about a sentimental nurse destroying all that for the sake of an ape-boy."

"*Ape-boy!*" said Miss Fellowes, in helpless fury.

"That's what the reporters would call him," said Hoskins.

One of the men emerged now, looping a nylon rope through eyelets along the upper portion of the wall.

Miss Fellowes remembered the rope that Hoskins had pulled outside the room containing Professor Ademewski's rock specimen so long ago.

She cried out, "No!"

But Hoskins put Timmie down and gently removed the overcoat he was wearing. "You stay here, Timmie. Nothing will happen to you. We're just going outside for a moment. All right?"

Timmie, white and wordless, managed to nod.

Hoskins steered Miss Fellowes out of the dollhouse ahead of himself. For a moment, Miss Fellowes was beyond resistance. Dully, she noticed the hand-pull being adjusted outside the dollhouse.

"I'm sorry, Miss Fellowes," said Hoskins. "I would have spared you this. I planned it for the night so that you would know only when it was over."

She said in a weary whisper, "Because your son was hurt. Because he tormented this child into striking out at him."

"No. Believe me. I understand about the incident today and I know it was Jerry's fault. But the story has leaked out. It would have to with the press surrounding us on this day of all days. I can't risk having a distorted story about negligence and savage Neanderthalers, so-called, distract from the success of Project Middle Ages. Timmie has to go soon anyway; he might as well go now and give the sensationalists as small a peg as possible on which to hang their trash."

"It's not like sending a rock back. You'll be killing a human being."

"Not killing. There'll be no sensation. He'll simply be a Neanderthal boy in a Neanderthal world. He will no longer be a prisoner and alien. He will have a chance at a free life."

"What chance? He's only seven years old, used to being taken care of, fed, clothed, sheltered. He will be alone. His tribe may not be at the point where he left them now that four years have passed. And if they were, they would not recognize him. He will have to take care of himself. How will he know how?"

Hoskins shook his head in hopeless negative. "Lord, Miss Fellowes, do you think we haven't thought of that? Do you think we would have brought in a child if it weren't that it was the first successful fix of a human or near-human we made and that we did not dare to take the chance of unfixing him and finding another fix as good? Why do you suppose we kept Timmie as long as we did, if it were not for our reluctance to send a child back into the past? It's just"—his voice took on a desperate urgency—"that we can wait no longer. Timmie stands in the way of expansion! Timmie is a source of possible bad publicity; we are on the threshold of great things, and I'm sorry, Miss Fellowes, but we can't let Timmie block us. We cannot. We cannot. I'm sorry, Miss Fellowes."

"Well, then," said Miss Fellowes sadly. "Let me say good-by. Give me five minutes to say good-by. Spare me that much."

Hoskins hesitated. "Go ahead."

Timmie ran to her. For the last time he ran to her and for the last time Miss Fellowes clasped him in her arms.

For a moment, she hugged him blindly. She caught at a chair with the toe of one foot, moved it against the wall, sat down.

"Don't be afraid, Timmie."

"I'm not afraid if you're here, Miss Fellowes. Is that man mad at me, the man out there?"

"No, he isn't. He just doesn't understand

about us. ——Timmie, do you know what a mother is?'

"Like Jerry's mother?"

"Did he tell you about his mother?"

"Sometimes. I think maybe a mother is a lady who takes care of you and who's very nice to you and who does good things."

"That's right. Have you ever wanted a mother, Timmie?"

Timmie pulled his head away from her so that he could look into her face. Slowly, he put his hand to her cheek and hair and stroked her, as long, long ago she had stroked him. He said, "Aren't you my mother?"

"Oh, Timmie."

"Are you angry because I asked?"

"No. Of course not."

"Because I know your name is Miss Fellowes, but—but sometimes, I call you 'Mother' inside. Is that all right?"

"Yes. Yes. It's all right. And I won't leave you any more and nothing will hurt you. I'll be with you to care for you always. Call me Mother, so I can hear you."

"Mother," said Timmie contentedly, leaning his cheek against hers.

She rose, and, still holding him, stepped up on the chair. The sudden beginning of a shout from outside went unheard and, with her free hand, she yanked with all her weight at the cord where it hung suspended between two eyelets.

And Stasis was punctured and the room was empty.

SPECIAL ENTRY IN FIELD EXPEDITION
[NOTEBOOK]:

Since it is now [my] intention to prefer charges against [my] [partner-teammate] [Smith] and to use these [notes] as a formal [document] in the matter, [I] shall now summarize in detail the particulars of the case:

[We] have been on Earth for [expression of time-units] on a field expedition to determine whether or not the dominant species here possesses the Synapse known to our [catalog] as Beta sub Sixteen, the master [computer] [at home] having concluded that without the Synapse, this Earth culture must become extinct.

On arrival [we] set up the usual [detectors], expecting to get our information in a [expression of very short time-unit] or so; but to our [great astonishment] the readings on the [kickshaw], the [gimmick] and the high-sensitivity [snivvy] were mixed; it appears that this culture possessed the Synapse but did not use it [!!!]

[I] submit that [Smith] is guilty of carelessness and [unethical] conduct. [I] see no solution but to destroy this specimen and perhaps the others. [I] declare that this situation has arisen because [Smith] ignored [my] clearly [stated] warning. As [I] [write], this alerted, frightened specimen stands ready to commit violence on [our] [equipment] and thereby itself. [I] hereby serve notice on [Smith] that [he] got [us] into this and [he] can [   ]ing well get [us] out.

The Tor Double Novels

A Meeting with Medusa by Arthur C. Clarke/*Green Mars* by Kim Stanley Robinson

Hardfought by Greg Bear/*Cascade Point* by Timothy Zahn

Born with the Dead by Robert Silverberg/*The Saliva Tree* by Brian W. Aldiss

No Truce with Kings by Poul Anderson/*Ship of Shadows* by Fritz Leiber

Enemy Mine by Barry B. Longyear/*Another Orphan* by John Kessel

Screwtop by Vonda N. McIntyre/*The Girl Who Was Plugged In* by James Tiptree, Jr.

The Nemesis from Terra by Leigh Brackett/*Battle for the Stars* by Edmond Hamilton

Sailing to Byzantium by Robert Silverberg/*Seven American Nights* by Gene Wolfe

Houston, Houston, Do You Read? by James Tiptree, Jr./*Souls* by Joanna Russ

He Who Shapes by Roger Zelazny/*The Infinity Box* by Kate Wilhelm

The Blind Geometer by Kim Stanley Robinson/*The New Atlantis* by Ursula K. Le Guin

* forthcoming

THEODORE STURGEON

A TOM DOHERTY ASSOCIATES BOOK
NEW YORK

THE [WIDGET], THE [WADGET], AND BOFF

Copyright © 1955 by Theodore Sturgeon

A TOR Book
Published by Tom Doherty Associates, Inc.
49 West 24 Street
New York, NY 10010

Cover design by Carol Russo

ISBN: 0-812-55966-5   Can. ISBN: 0-812-55973-8

First Tor edition: June 1989

Printed in the United States of America

0 9 8 7 6 5 4 3 2 1

PART ONE

THROUGHOUT THE CONTINUUM as we know it (and a good deal more, as we don't know it) there are cultures that fly and cultures that swim; there are boron folk and flourine fellowships, cupro-coprophages and (roughly speaking) immaterial life-forms which swim and swirl around each other in space like so many pelagic shards of metaphysics. And some organize into super-entities like a beehive or a slime-mold so that they live plurally to become singular, and some have even more singular ideas of plurality.

Now, no matter how an organized culture of intelligent beings is put together or where, re-gardless of what it's made of or how it lives, there is one thing all cultures have in common, and it is the most obvious of traits. There are as many names for it as there are cultures, of course, but in all it works the same way—the same way the inner ear functions (with its con-tributory synapses) in a human being when he steps on Junior's roller skate. He doesn't think about how far away the wall is, some wires or your wife, or in which direction: he *grabs*, and, more often than not, he *gets*—accurately and without analysis. Just so does an individual re-

flexively adjust when imbalanced in his socio-
cultural matrix: he experiences the reflex of reflexes, a thing as large as the legendary view
afforded a drowning man of his entire past, in
a single illuminated instant wherein the mind
moves, as it were, at right angles to time and
travels high and far for its survey.

And this is true of every culture everywhere,
the cosmos over. So obvious and necessary a
thing is seldom examined: but it was once, by a
culture which called this super-reflex "Synapse
Beta sub Sixteen."

What came out of the calculator surprised
them. They were, after all, expecting an answer.

Human eyes would never have recognized the
device for what it was. Its memory bank was an
atomic cloud, each particle of which was sealed
away from the others by a self-sustaining en-
velope of force. Subtle differences in nuclei, in
probability shells, and in internal tensions were
the coding, and fields of almost infinite varia-
bility were used to call up the particles in the
desired combinations. These were channeled in
a way beyond description in earthly mathematics, detected by a principle as yet unknown to
us, and translated into language (or, more accurately, an analog of what we understand as
language). Since this happened so far away,
temporally, spatially, and culturally, proper
nouns are hardly proper; it suffices to say that
it yielded results, in this particular setting,
which were surprising. These were correlated
into a report, the gist of which was this:

Prognosis positive, or prognosis negative, de-

pending upon presence or absence of Synapse Beta sub Sixteen.

The pertinent catalog listed the synapse in question as "indetectible except by field survey." Therefore an expedition was sent.

All of which may seem fairly remote until one realizes that the prognosis was being drawn for that youthful and dangerous aggregate of bubbling yeasts called "human culture," and that when the term "prognosis negative" was used it meant *finis*, the end, zero, *ne plus ultra* altogether.

It must be understood that the possessors of the calculator, the personnel of the expedition to Earth, were not Watchers in the Sky and Arbiters of Our Fate. Living in our midst, here and now, is a man who occupies himself with the weight-gain of amebæ from their natal instant to the moment they fission. There is a man who, having produced neurosis in cats, turns them into alcoholics for study. Someone has at long last settled the matter of the camel's capacity for, and retention of, water. People like these are innocent of designs on the destinies of *all* amebæ, cats, camels and cultures; there are simply certain things they want to *know*. This is the case no matter how unusual, elaborate, or ingenious their methods might be. So—an expedition came here for information.

EXCERPT FROM FIELD EXPEDITION [NOTE-BOOK][1].
[VOLUME] ONE:

CONCLUSION. . . . to restate the obvious, [we]
have been on Earth long enough and more than
long enough to have discovered anything and
everything [we] [wished] about any [sensible-
predictible-readable] culture anywhere. This
one, however, is quite beyond [understanding-
accounting-for]. At first sight, [one] was
tempted to conclude immediately that it possesses the Synapse, because no previously
known culture has advanced to this degree
without it, ergo . . . And then [we] checked it
with [our] [instruments] [! ! !] [Our] [gimmick]
and our [kickshaw] gave [us] absolutely negative readings, so [we] activated a high-
sensitivity [snivvy] and got results which
approximate nonsense: the Synapse is scattered through the population randomly, here

[1]*TRANSLATOR'S NOTE: Despite the acknowledged fact
that the translator is an expert on extraterrestrial language, culture, philosophy, and the theory and design
of xenological devices, the reader's indulgence is re-
quested in this instance. To go into detail about these
machines and the nature and modes of communication
of the beings that operate them would be like writing
the story of a young lover on the way to his reward,
springing up his beloved's front steps, ringing the bell—
and then stopping to present explicit detail about cir-
cuitous wiring and dry, dry cells. It is deemed more
direct and more economical to use loose and convenient translations and to indicate them by brackets, in
order to confine the narrative to the subject at hand.
Besides, it pleases the translator's modesty to be so
sparing with his [omniscience].*

non-existent or dormant, there in brief full ac-
tivity at [unheard-of] high levels. [I] thought
[Smith] would go [out of [his] mind] and as for
[myself], [I] had a crippling attack of the [   ]s
at the very concept. More for [our] own protec-
tion than for the furtherance of the Expedition,
[we] submitted all our data to [our] [ship]'s
[computer] and got what appeared to be even
further nonsense: the conclusion that this species possesses the Synapse but to all intents
and purposes does not use it.
How can a species possess Synapse Beta sub
Sixteen and not use it? Nonsense, nonsense,
nonsense!
So complex and contradictory are [our] data
that [we] can only fall back on a microcosmic
analysis and proceed by its guidance. [We]
shall therefore isolate a group of specimens
under [laboratory] control, even though it
means using a [miserable] [primitive] [battery]-
powered [wadget]. [We]'ll put our new-model
[widget] on the job, too. [We]'ve had enough
of this [uncanny, uncomfortable] feeling of
standing in the presence of [apology-for-
obscenity] paradox.

I

The town was old enough to have slums, large
enough to have no specific "tracks" with a right
and a wrong side. Its nature was such that a
boarding house could, without being unusual,
contain such varied rungs on the social ladder
as a young, widowed night-club hostess and her
three-year-old son; a very good vocational guid-

ance expert; a young law clerk; the librarian from the high school; and a stage-struck maiden from a very small small town. They said Sam Bittelman, who nominally owned and operated the boarding house, could have been an engineer, and if he had been, a marine architect as well, but instead he had never risen higher than shop foreman. Whether this constituted failure or success is speculative; apply to a chief petty officer or top sergeant who won't accept a commission, and to the president of your local bank, and take your pick of their arguments. It probably never occurred to Sam to examine the matter. He had other things to amuse him. Tolerant, curious, intensely alive, old Sam had apparently never retired from anything but his job at the shipyards back east.

He in turn was owned and operated by his wife, whom everyone called "Bitty" and who possessed the harshest countenance and the most acid idiom ever found in a charter member of the Suckers for Sick Kittens and Sob Stories Society. Between them they took care of their roomers in that special way possible only in boarding houses which feature a big dining table and a place set for everyone. Such places are less than a family, or more if you value your freedom. They are more than a hotel, or less if you like formality. To Mary Haunt, who claimed to be twenty-two and lied, the place was the most forgettable and soon-to-be-forgotten of stepping stones; to Robin it was home and more; it was the world and the universe, an environment as ubiquitous, unnoticed, and unquestioned as the water around a fish; but Robin

would, of course, feel differently later. He was
only three. The only other one of the Bittelmans' boarders who breathed what was
uniquely the Bittelman quality as if it were air
was Phil Halvorsen, a thoughtful young man in
the vocational guidance field, whose mind was
on food and housing only when they annoyed
him, and since the Bittelmans made him quite
comfortable, in effect they were invisible. Reta
Schmidt appreciated the Bittelmans for a number of things, prime among which was the
lengths to which her dollar went with them, for
Miss Schmidt's employers were a Board of Education. Mr. Anthony O'Banion permitted himself a genuine admiration of almost nothing in
these parts. So it remained for Sue Martin to
be the only one in the place who respected and
admired them, right from the start, with something approaching their due. Sue was Robin's
widowed mother and worked in a night club as
hostess and sometime entertainer. She had
done, in the past, both better and worse. She
still might do better for herself, but only that
which would be worse for Robin. The Bittelmans were her godsend. Robin adored them,
and the only thing they would not do for him
was to spoil him. The Bittelmans were there to
give him breakfast in the mornings, to dress
him when he went out to play, to watch over
him and keep him amused and content until Sue
rose at 11. The rest of the day was for Sue and
Robin together, right up to his bedtime, when
she tucked him in and storied him to sleep. And
when she left for work at 9 P.M., the Bittelmans
were there, safe and certain, ready and willing

to cope with anything from a bladder to a blaze.
They were like insurance and fire extinguish-
ers, hardly ever used but comforting by their
presence. So she valued them . . . but then, Sue
Martin was different from most people. So was
Robin; however, this is a truism when speaking
of three-year-olds.

Such was the population of Bittelman's
boarding house, and if they seem too many and
too varied to sort out all at once, have patience
and remember that each of them felt the same
way on meeting all the others.

II

A pawnshop is a dismal place.

A pawnshop in the rain. A closed pawnshop
in the rain, on a Sunday.

Philip Halvorsen did not object. He had a lik-
ing for harmony, and the atmosphere suited
him well just now, his thoughts, his feelings. A
sunbeam would have been an intrusion. A
flower shop could not have contributed so
much. People, just now, would have been intol-
erable.

He leaned his forehead against the wet black
steel of the burglar-proof gate and idly inven-
toried the contents of the window and his
thoughts about them. Like the window and its
contents, and the dark recesses inside, his
thoughts were miscellaneous, cluttered, captured in that purgatory of uselessness wherein
things are not dead, only finished with what
they have been and uncaring of what will happen to them and when. His thoughts were bin-

oculars without eyes, cameras without film, silent guitars and unwound watches.

He found himself approving more of the guitars than the two dirty violins hanging in the window. He almost wondered why this should be, almost let the question disappear into lethargy, and at last sighed and ran the matter down because he knew it would bother him otherwise and he was in no mood to be bothered. He looked at the instruments lazily, one, the other, analyzing and comparing. They had a great deal in common, and some significant differences. Having a somewhat sticky mind, to which windblown oddments of fact had been adhering for nearly 30 years now, he knew of the trial-and-error evolution of those resonance-chambers and of the high degree of perfection they had come to. Given that design followed function in both the violin and the guitar, and aside from any preference in the sounds they made (actually Halvorsen was completely indifferent to music anyway), then why should he intuitively prefer the guitars he saw over the violins? Size, proportion, number of strings, design of bridge, frets or lack of them, finish, peg and tailpiece mechanics—all these had their differences and all were perfect for the work they did.

Suddenly, then, he saw it, and his mind swiftly thumbed through the mental pictures of all the violins he had ever seen. They all checked out. One flickering glance at the guitars in the window settled the matter.

All violins have a scroll carved at the end of the neck—*all* of them. There is scrollwork on

some guitars, none on others; it's obviously optional. The back-bending spiral at the end of a
violin's neck is not optional, but traditional, and
it has no function. Halvorsen nodded slightly
and permitted his mind to wander away from
the matter. It wasn't important—not in itself;
only settling it was important. His original, in-
tuitive approval of guitars over violins was not
a matter of moment either; his preference for
the functional over the purely traditional was
just that—a preference.

None of this required much of Halvorsen's
conscious effort or attention. The survey, the
sequence, was virtually reflexive, and his
thoughts moved as fish in some deep clear pool
might move, hanging and hanging, fanning, then
suddenly darting about with a swirl and a
splash, to hang again fanning, alive and waiting.

He stood motionless, the fine rain soaking
into the back of his collar and his eyes unseek-
ing but receptive. Binoculars with mother-of-
pearl; binoculars without. A watch with glass
rubies in the face. Display cards: cheap combs,
cheap wallets, cheap pens. An electric steam
iron with a frayed cord. A rack of second-hand
clothing.

Guns.

He felt again that vague dissatisfaction, set
up a certain amount of lethargic resistance to
it, and when it came through anyway he pa-
tiently gave it its head. He looked at the guns.
What bothered him about the guns?

One had a pearl handle and rococo etching
along the barrel, but that wasn't it. He glanced

down the row and settled on a .38 automatic, about as functional an artifact as could be imagined—small, square, here knurled and there polished, with the palm safety and lock-safety just where they should be. And still he felt that faint disapproval, that dissatisfaction that spelt criticism. He widened his scan to all the guns, and felt it just as much. Just as little.

It was categorical then. It had to do with all these guns, or with all guns. He looked again, and again, and within this scope found no crevice for the prying of his reason, so he turned the problem on its back and looked again: what would a gun be like if it satisfied this fastidious intuition of his?

It came in a flash, and he hardly believed it: a flimsy structure of rolled sheet metal with a simple firing pin on a piece hinged and sprung like the business part of a rattrap. There was no butt, there were no sights. No trigger either; just a simple catch and—what was that?—and a piece of string. He visualized it sitting on a polished surface on a wire stand, its thin barrel angled upwards about 45°, like a toy cannon. Its caliber was about .38. The feature which struck him most was the feeling of fragility, lightness, in the whole design. Design! What would an object like that be designed *for*?

He looked again at the pawned guns. Among the things they had in common was massiveness. Breeches were cast steel, muzzles thick-walled, probably all rifled; parts were tempered, hardened, milled, designed and built to contain and direct repeated explosions, repeated internal assaults by hot hurtling metal.

It was as if a little red signal-light flickered on the concept *repeated*. Was that it, that all these guns were designed for repeated use? Was he dissatisfied with that? Why?

He conjured up the image of a single-shot dueling pistol he had once handled: long-barreled, muzzle-loading, with a powder-pan for priming and a chip of flint fixed to the hammer. To his surprise he found the little metal red light still aflicker; this was a design that displeased him too, somewhere in the area labeled *repeated*.

Even a single-shot pistol was designed to be used over again; that must be it. Then to him, a gun satisfied its true function only if it was designed to be used only once. *Enough* is the criterion of optimum design, and in this case once was enough.

Halvorsen snorted angrily. He disliked being led by rational means to a patently irrational conclusion. He cast back over his reasoning, looking for the particular crossroads where he must have taken a wrong turning.

There was none.

At this point his leisurely, almost self-powered curiosity was replaced by an incandescent ferocity of examination. Logic burned in Halvorsen as fury did in other men, and he had no tolerance for the irrational. He attacked it as a personal indignity, and would not let up until he had wrapped it up, tied it down, in the fabric of his understanding.

He let himself visualize the "gun" of his satisfied imagination, with its mousetrap firing mechanism, its piece of string, its almost useless flimsiness, and for a moment pictured po-

lice, cattlemen, Army officers handling such a ridiculous object. But the vison dissolved and he shook his head; the guns ordinarily used by such people satisfied his sense of function perfectly. He slipped (hypothetically) into the consciousness of such a man and regarded his gun—*a* gun—any gun with satisfaction. No, this seemed a personal matter, unlike the dissatisfaction everyone should feel (if they cared) about the extraordinary fact that automobiles are streamlined only where they show, and are powered by a heat-engine which is inoperable without a cooling system.

What's so special about my mousetrap gun? he demanded of himself, and turned his eye inward to look at it again. There it sat, on a polished surface—table-top, was it?—with its silly piece of string leading forward toward him and its muzzle tilted upward, unabashedly showing off its sleazy construction.

Why could he see how thin the metal of that muzzle was?

Because it was aimed right at the bridge of his nose.

·Make a statement, Halvorsen, and test it. Statement: Other guns satisfy other men because they can be used over and over again. This gun satisfies me because it goes off once, and once is enough.

Test: A dueling pistol goes off only once; yet it can be reloaded and used again. Why not this? Answer: Because whoever uses a dueling pistol expects to be able to use it again. Whoever sees it used expects it will be used again, because the world goes on.

After Halvorsen's mousetrap gun went off, the world wouldn't go on. Not for Halvorsen—which of course is the same thing. "I am the core and the center of the universe" is a fair statement for anyone.

So restate, and conclude: The optimum gun design is that which, having shot Halvorsen between the eyes, need no longer exist. Since *optimum* carried with it the flavor of *preferred performance*, it is fair to state that within himself Halvorsen found a preference for being shot to death. More specifically, for dying. Correction: for being dead—gladly.

Momentarily, Halvorsen felt such pleasure at having solved his problem that he neglected to look at the solution, and when he did, it chilled him far more than the fine rain could.

Why should he want to be dead?

He glanced at the racked guns in the pawnshop and saw them as if for the first time, each one very real and genuinely menacing. He shuddered, clung for a moment to the wet black steel of the gate, then abruptly turned away.

In all his thoughtful—thought-*filled*—life he had never consciously entertained such a concept. Perhaps this was because he was a receptive person rather than a transmissive one. What he collected he used on his external world –his job—rather than on himself. He had no need for the explanations and apologies, the interpretations and demands-to-be-heard of the outgoing person, so he had no need to indulge in self-seeking and the complicated semantics of ego-translation. He was rather a clearinghouse for the facts he found, taking knowledge

and experience from *here* and storing them virtually untouched until they could be applied *there*.

He walked slowly homeward, in a state that would be numbness except for the whirling, wondering core which turned and poked and worried at this revelation. Why should he want to be dead?

Philip Halvorsen loved being alive. Correction: He enjoyed being alive. (Question: Why the correction? File for later.) He was a vocational guidance worker employed by a national social service organization. He was paid what he should be, according to his sense of values, and thanks to the Bittelmans he lived a little better on it than he might otherwise. He did not work for money, anyway; his work was a way of thinking, a way of life. He found it intriguing, engrossing, deeply satisfying. Each applicant was a challenge, each placement a victory over one or more of the enemies that plague mankind—insecurity, inferiority, blindness and ignorance. Each time he looked up from his desk and saw a new applicant entering his cubicle, he experienced a strange silent excitement. It was a pressure, a power, like flicking on the master switch of a computing machine; he sat there with all relays open and all circuits blank, waiting for the answers to those first two questions: "What are you doing now?" and "What do you want to do?" Just that; it was enough for that indefinable sense of satisfaction or dissatisfaction to make itself known to him. And just as he had analyzed its source in the matter of guns, so he analyzed his clients. That flick-

ering light signaling wrongness, misapplica-
tion, malfunction, misevaluation—all the flaws
in design, the false goals, the frustrations and
hurts of those who wonder if they have chosen
the right vocation- -that light burned on while
he worked on each case, and would not go out
until he found the answer. Once or twice he had
wished, whimsically, that his imagined signal
light would illuminate a sign for the client
which said *Steeplejack* and for that one which
said *Frog Farmer*, but it refused to be so oblig-
ing. It only told him when he was wrong. Being
right involved laborious and meticulous work,
but he did it gladly. And when at last he was
satisfied, he frequently found that his work had
just begun: to tell an eighty-dollar-a-week bank
clerk that his proper niche is in freight-handling
with a two-year apprenticeship at 50 is initially
a thankless task. But Halvorsen knew how to
be quiet and wait, and had become a past master at the art of letting a client fight himself,
defeat himself, reconstruct himself, and at last
persuade himself that the vocational counsellor
was right. And all of it, Halvorsen liked, from
the challenge to the accomplishment. Why, why
should there be a wish in him to have this cease,
to end the world in which all these intriguing
problems existed? And to be glad of its ending?

What would he advise a client, a stranger, if
that stranger blurted out such a desire?

Well, he wouldn't. It would depend. He would
simply throw that in with everything else about
the client—age, education, temperament, mari-
tal status, I.Q., and all the rest of it, and let the
death-wish throw its weight along with all the

other factors. It would, however, predispose him to conclude that the man was intolerably misplaced in some area: in a marriage, a family situation, a social beartrap of some kind . . . or his job. His job. Was he, Halvorsen, judge and arbiter of occupations—was he in the wrong job?

He slouched along in the rain, huddled down into himself to escape a far more penetrating chill than this drenching mist. So uncharacteristically wrapped in his inward thought was he that he had taken three steps on dry pavement before he became aware of it. He stopped and took his bearings.

He stood under the marquee of the smallest and cheapest of the town's four theaters. It was closed and dark, this being Sunday in a "blue-law" district, but dead bulbs and locked doors did not modify the shrillness of its decorations. Over the main entrance were two groups of huge letters, one for each of the two features on the bill. SIN FOR SALE, one shrieked, and the other blared back SLAVES OF THE HELL-FLOWER. Under these was a third sign, offering as a special added attraction *Love Rites of a South Sea Eden.* From the sidewalk on the far left, up to the marquee, across and down the other side was an arch of cardboard cut-outs of women, wilting and wet, unnaturally proportioned and inhumanly posed, with scraps of ribbon and drape, locks of hair and induced shadows performing a sort of indicative concealment on their unbelievable bodies. Over the box-office was the stern advice: *Adults only!!!* and papering the supporting pillars just inside

the mirrored cavern of a lobby were still pho-
tographs of highlights of the pictures: A bare-
backed female with her hands trussed to a high
tree-branch, being whipped; a man standing,
gun in hand, over a delectable corpse whose
head hung back and down over the edge of the
bed so that her carefully arranged hair swept
the floor, and some flyblown samples of the
South Sea Eden with the portraits of its inhab-
itants smeared strategically with rubber-stamp
ink in angry and careless obedience to some local by-law.

At the best of times this sort of display left
Phil Halvorsen cold. At the worst of times (up
to now) he would have felt a mild disgust leav-
ened by enough amusement at the outhouse
crudity of it to make it supportable—and forgettable. But at the moment things were a little
worse than the worst had ever been before. It
was as if his earlier unpleasant revelation had
in some obscure way softened him up, opened
a seam in a totally unexpected place in his ar-
mor. The display smote him like a blast of heat.
He blinked and stepped back a pace, half-raising
his hands and screwing his eyes shut. Behind
the lids, the picture of his ridiculous one-shot
cannon rose up roaring. He thought he could
see a bullet emerging from its smoking muzzle
like the tip of a hot black tongue. He shuddered
away from the millisecond nightmare and
opened his eyes, only to get a second and even
more overwhelming reaction from the theater-
front.

My God, what's happening to me? he silently
screamed to himself. He pounded his forehead

with his fists twice, then put his head down and
ran up the street, up the hill. His photographic
eye had picked up the banner inside the lobby,
and as he ran, part of him coldly read it:

SEE (in flaming scarlet) the big-city orgies.
SEE the temptation of a teen-ager.
SEE lust run riot.
SEE the uncensored rites of an island cult.
SEE. . . . SEE. . . . There was more. As he ran,
he moaned.

And then he thought, at the Bittelmans there
are people, it is light, it is warm, it is almost
home.

He began to run to something instead of
away.

III

The Bittelmans' kitchen was a vague "back-
stairs" area to O'Banion and a functional ad-
junct of the boarding house to Halvorsen; to
Miss Schmidt it was forbidden ground which
excited no special interest for that—almost all
the world was forbidden ground to Miss
Schmidt. In it Sue Martin was as content as she
was anywhere, and among the torments of Mary
Haunt, the kitchen was a special hell. But in
Robin's world it was central, more so than the
bedroom he shared with his mother, more so
than his crib. He ate in the kitchen, played there
when it was raining or especially cold. When he
went outdoors it was through the kitchen door,
and it was a place to come back to with a
bruised knee, with a hollow stomach, with a
sudden flood of loneliness or of a three-year-

old's wild manic passion. It was big and warm and full of friends.

The most resourceful of these friends was, of course, Bitty, who without ever losing her gruff-ness knew the right time to apply a cookie or a story (usually about a little boy with a beautiful mother) or a swat on the bottom. Sam was a friend, too, mostly as something safe to climb on. Of late, O'Banion had carved a rather special niche for himself, and Robin had always liked a limited amount of Miss Schmidt's self-conscious passiveness; she was a wonderful listener. He treated Halvorsen with cheerful respect, and Mary Haunt as if she did not exist. There were other people, too, every bit as much so as anyone who ate and had a job and occupied rooms elsewhere in the house. There was the electric mixer and the washing machine—in Robin's economical language "Washeen"—the blendor and the coffeepot; in short, everything which had a motor in it. (The presence or absence of motors in percolators is arguable only by those with preconceptions.) To him they were all alive, responsive and articulate, and he held converse with them all. He showed them his toys and he told them the news, he bade them goodby and good morning, hello, what's the matter, and happy birthday.

And besides all these people, there were Boff and Georgie, who, though by no means limited to the kitchen, were often there.

They were not there on that dark Sunday while the sky grieved and Halvorsen fought his personal devils outdoors. "Mits-ter, Boff an' Googie gone for ride," Robin informed the elec-

tric mixer. Its name, Mits-ter, was identical in his vocabulary with "Mister" and was a clear link between the machine and the males he heard spoken of, and just another proof of the living personality he assigned to it. He got a kitchen chair and carried it effortfully over to the work-table, where he put it down and climbed on it. He tilted the mixer up and back and turned its control-cowling, and it began to hum softly. Bitty kept the beaters in a high drawer well out of his reach and let him play with the therefore harmless machine to his heart's content. "*Ats* right, Mitster," he crooned. "Eat your yunch. Hey, Washeen!" he called to the washing-machine, "Mitster's eatin' his yunch all up, I go' give him a cookie, he's a *good* boy." He revved the control up and down, the machine whining obediently. He spun the turntable, turned the motor off, listened to the ball-bearings clicking away in the turntable, stopped it and turned on the motor again. He turned suddenly at the nudge of some sixth sense and saw O'Banion in the doorway. "Goo' morning Tonio," he called, beaming. "Go picnic now?"

"Not today, it's raining," said O'Banion, "and it's 'good afternoon' now." He crossed to the table. "What you up to, fellow?"

"Mitster eatin' his yunch."

"Your mother asleep?"

"Yis."

O'Banion stood watching the child's complete preoccupation with the machine. Little son of a gun, he thought, how did you do it?

The question was all he could express about the strangely rewarding friendship which flow-

ered between him and Robin. He had never liked (nor, for that matter, disliked) a child in his life. He had never been exposed to one before; his only sibling was an older sister and he had never associated with anyone but contemporaries since he was a child himself.

Robin had caught him alone one day and had demanded to know his name. "Tony O'Banion," he had growled reluctantly. "Tonio?" "Tony O'Banion," he had corrected distinctly. "Tonio," Robin had said positively, and from then on that was inalterably that. And surprisingly, O'Banion had come to like it. And when, on the outskirts of town, someone had set up something called a Kiddie Karnival, a sort of miniature amusement park, and he had been assigned to handle land rentals there for his firm, he found himself thinking of Robin every time he saw the place, and of the Karnival every time he saw Robin, until one warm Sunday he startled himself and everyone else concerned by asking Sue Martin if he could take the boy there. She had looked at him gravely for a moment and said, "Why?"

"I think he might like it."

"Well, thanks," she had said warmly, "I think that's wonderful." And so he and Robin had gone.

And they'd gone again, several times, mostly on Sundays when Sue Martin was taking her one luxurious afternoon nap of the week, but a couple of times during the week too, when O'Banion had business out there and could conveniently pick the child up on the way out from the office and drop him again on the way back.

And then, just for a change, a picnic, Robin's very first, by the bank of a brook where they had watched jewel-eyed baby frogs and darting minnows and a terrifying miniature monster that he later identified as a dragonfly nymph; and Robin had asked so many questions that he had gone to a bookstore the next day and bought a bird book and a wildflower guide.

Occasionally he asked himself *why?* What was he getting out of it? and found the answers either uncomfortable or elusive. Perhaps it was the relaxation: for the first time he could have communion with another human being without the cautious and watchful attention he usually paid to "Where did you go to school?" and "Who are your people?" Perhaps it was the warmth of friendship radiating from a face so disturbingly like the one which still intruded itself between his eyes and his work once in a while, and which was so masked and controlled when he encountered it in the flesh.

And there had been the Sunday when Sue Martin, after having given her permission for one of these outings, had suddenly said, "I haven't much to do this afternoon. Are these excursions of yours strictly stag?" "Yes," he had said immediately, "they are." He'd told *her.* But—it didn't feel like a victory, and she had not seemed defeated when she shrugged and smiled and said, "Let me know when you go coeducational." After that she didn't put a stop to the picnics, either, which would have pleased him by permitting him to resent her. He found himself wishing she would ask again, but he knew she would not, not ever. And if he should ask

her to come, and she should refuse . . . he could
not bear the thought. Sometimes he thought the
whole business of amusing the child was done
to impress the mother; he had overheard Mary
Haunt make a remark to Miss Schmidt once
that intimated as much, and had furiously
sworn off for all of six hours, which was when
Robin asked him where they would go next. As
long as it was simple, a matter between him
and the child, it required no excuses or explanations. As soon as he placed the matter in any
matrix, he became confused and uncertain. He
therefore avoided analyses, and asked himself
admiringly and academically, little son of a gun,
how did you do it? while he watched Robin's
animated conversation with the electric mixer.

He rumpled Robin's hair and went to the
stove, where he picked up the coffeepot and
swirled it. It was almost full, and he lit the gas
under it.

"Wha' you do, Tonio? Make coffee?"

"Yea bo."

"Okay," said Robin, as if granting permission. "Boff doesn't drink coffee, Tonio," he con-
fided. "Oh no."

"He doesn't, hm?" O'Banion looked around
and up. "Is Boff here?"

"No," said Robin. "He not here."

"Where'd he go? Out with the Bittelmans?"

"Yis." The coffeepot grumbled and Robin
said, "*Hello*, Coffeepot."

Halvorsen came in and stood blindly in the
doorway. O'Banion looked up and greeted him,
then said under his breath, "My God!" and
crossed the room. "You all right, Halvorsen?"

Halvorsen directed blind eyes at the sound of his voice, and O'Banion could watch seeing enter them slowly, like the fade-in on a movie screen. "What?" His face was wet with the rain, fish-belly pale, and he stood slumping like a man with a weight on his back, raising his face to look up rather than lifting his head.

"You'd better sit down," said O'Banion. He told himself that this unwonted concern for the tribulations of a fellow-human was purely a selfish matter of not wanting to shovel the stunned creature up off the floor. Yet as Halvorsen turned toward the ell with its wooden chairs, O'Banion caught at the open front of Halvorsen's coat. "Let me take this, it's sopping."

"No," said Halvorsen. "No." But he let O'Banion take the coat; rather, he walked out of it, leaving O'Banion with it foolishly in his hands. O'Banion cast about him, then hung it up on the broom-hook and turned again to Halvorsen, who had just fallen heavily back into a chair.

Again Halvorsen went through that slow transition from blindness to sight, from isolation to awareness. He made some difficult, internal effort and then said, "Supper ready?"

"We roll our own," said O'Banion. "Bitty and Sam are taking their once-a-month trip to the fleshpots."

"Fleshpots," said Robin, without turning his head.

Carefully controlling his face and his voice, O'Banion continued, "They said to raid the refrigerator, only hands off the leg o' lamb, that's for tomorrow." Motioning toward Robin with

his head, he added, "He doesn't miss a trick," and at last released a broad grin.

Halvorsen said, "I'm not hungry."

"I've got some coffee going."

"Good."

O'Banion dropped a round asbestos mat on the table and went for the coffeepot. On the way back he got a cup and saucer. He put them on the table and sat down. Sugar was already there; spoons were in a tumbler, handles down, country-style. He poured and added sugar and stirred. He looked across at Halvorsen, and saw something on that reserved face that he had read about but had never seen before; the man's lips were blue. Only then did it occur to him to get a cup for Halvorsen. He went for it, and remembered milk, too, just in case. He brought them back, hesitated, and then poured the second cup. He put a spoon in the saucer, and with sudden shyness pushed it and the milk toward the other man. "Hey!"

"What?" Halvorsen said in the same dead, flat tone, and "Oh. Oh! Thanks, O'Banion, thanks very I'm sorry." Suddenly he laughed forcefully and without mirth. He covered his eyes and said plaintively, "What's the *matter* with me?"

It was a question neither could answer, and they sat sipping coffee uncomfortably, a man who didn't know how to unburden himself and a man who had never taken up another's burden. Into this tableau walked Mary Haunt. She had on a startling yellow hostess gown and had a magazine tucked under her arm. She threw one swift gaze around the room and curled her lip.

"Grand Central Station," she growled and walked out.

O'Banion's anger came as a great relief to him at just that moment; he was almost grateful to the girl. "One of these days someone's going to grab that kid by the scruff of the neck and housebreak her," he snorted.

Halvorsen found a voice, too, and probably was as grateful for the change in focus. "It won't last," he said.

"What do you mean?"

"I mean she can't go on that way much longer," said Halvorsen thoughtfully. He paused and closed his eyes; O'Banion could see him pulling himself hand over hand out of his personal swamp, moving to dry ground, high ground, where he could look with familiarity at a real world again. When he opened his eyes he gave O'Banion a strange little smile and said, as if in parenthesis, "Thanks for the coffee, O'Banion," and went on: "She's waiting for the Big Break. She thinks she deserves it and that it will come to her if she only waits. She really believes that. You've heard of high-school kids who perch on drugstore stools hoping for a movie scout to come along and discover them. That's harmless as long as they do it an hour or two a day. But Mary Haunt does it every minute she's out of this house. None of us here could help her, so she treats us the way anyone treats useless things. But you ought to see her down at the station."

"What station?"

"She types continuities at the radio station," said Halvorsen. "From what I hear, she's not

very good, but on the other hand they don't pay
her much money, so nobody kicks. But to her a
radio station is the edge of the world she wants
to crash—it starts there and goes to TV and to
the movies. I'll bet you anything you like she
has a scene all rehearsed in her mind, where a
big producer or director stops here and drops
in at the radio station to see someone, and *bang!*
our Mary's a starlet being groomed for the top."

"She'd better learn some manners," grumbled O'Banion.

"Oh, she's got manners when she thinks
they'll do her some good."

"Why doesn't she use them on you, for example?"

"Me?"

"Yes. Don't you get people better jobs, that
sort of thing?"

"I see a lot of people, a lot of different kinds
of people," said Halvorsen, "but they have one
thing in common: they aren't sure what they
want to do, to be." He pointed his spoon at the
doorway. "She is. She may be wrong, but she's
certain."

"Well, what about Sue Martin?" said O'Banion. He pursued the subject quickly, almost
thoughtlessly, because of a vague feeling that if
he didn't, Halvorsen would slip back into that
uncomfortable introspective silence. "Surely
there's a lot about show business Mary Haunt
could learn from her."

Halvorsen gave the nearest thing yet to a grin
and reached for the coffeepot. "Mrs. Martin's a
nightclub entertainer," he said, "and as far as

Mary Haunt's concerned, night clubs are slums."

O'Banion blushed violently and cursed himself for it. "Why that little—no background, no—no—how could *she* look down on ... I mean, she's a little *nobody!*" Conscious that he was spluttering under the direct and passionless gaze of Halvorsen's dark eyes, he reached for the first thing he could think of that was not an absolute non sequitur: "One night a couple of months ago Mrs. Martin and I saw her throw a fit of hysterics over something ... oh, Miss Schmidt had a magazine she wanted ... anyway, after it was all over, Mrs. Martin said something about Mary Haunt that could have been a compliment. I mean, to some people. I can't think of Mary Haunt ever doing as much for her."

"What did she say?"

"Mrs. Martin? Oh, she said anybody who gets between Mary Haunt and what she wants is going to have a Mary-sized hole through them."

"It wasn't a compliment," said Halvorsen immediately. "Mrs. Martin knows as well as you or I do what's between that girl and her Big Break."

"What is?"

"Mary Haunt."

O'Banion thought about that for a moment and then chuckled. "A Mary-sized hole wouldn't leave much." He looked up. "You're quite a psychologist."

"Me?" said Halvorsen in genuine surprise. At that moment Robin, who had all this while been murmuring confidences to the mixer, switched

off the machine and looked up. "Boff!" he cried
joyously. "Hello, *Boff*!" He watched something
move toward him, turning slightly to follow it
with his eyes until it settled on the spice shelf
over his table. "Wash you doin', Boff? Come for
dinner?" Then he laughed, as if he had thought
of something pleasant and very funny.

"I thought Boff was out with the Bittelmans,
Robin," O'Banion called.

"No, he hide," said Robin, and laughed up-
roariously. "Boff right here. He come back."

Halvorsen watched this with a dazed smile.
"Who on earth is Boff?" he asked O'Banion.

"Imaginary playmate," said O'Banion knowl-
edgeably. "I'm used to it now but I don't mind
telling you it gave me the creeps at first. Lots
of kids have them. My sister did, or so Mother
says—Sister doesn't remember it now. A little
girl called Ginny who used to live in the butler's
pantry. You laugh off this 'Boff' and the other
one—her name's Googie—until you see Robin
holding the door open to let them in, or refusing to go out to play until they get downstairs.
And he isn't kidding. That's a nice little kid most
of the time, Halvorsen, but some things will
make him blow up like a little bottle of nitro,
and one of 'em is to deny that Boff and Googie
are real. I know. I tried it once and it took half
a day and six rides on a merry-go-round to calm
him down." He emphasized with a forefinger:
"Six rides for Boff and Googie too."

Halvorsen watched the child: "I'll be darned."
He shook his head slightly. "Is that—un-
healthy?"

"I bought a book," said O'Banion, and, unac-

countably, found himself blushing again, "and it says no, long as the child has good contact with reality, and believe me, he has. They grow out of it. Nothing to worry about."

Just then Robin cocked his head up to the spice shelf, as if he had heard a sound. Then he said, "Okay, Boff," climbed down from his chair, carried the chair across the kitchen to its place against the wall, and said cheerfully, "Tonio, Boff wan see cars. Okay. Shall we?"

O'Banion rose, laughing. "My master's voice. I got the *Popular Electrics* special issue on this year's automobiles and Boff and Robin can't get enough of it."

"Oh?" Halvorsen smiled. "What do they like this year?"

"Red ones. Come on, Robin. See you, Halvorsen."

"See you."

Robin trotted after O'Banion, paused near the door. "Come *on*, Boff!"

He waved violently at Halvorsen. "See you. Have-sum-gum."

Halvorsen waved back, and they were gone.

Halvorsen sat numbly for a while, his hand still raised. The presence of the other man and the child had been a diversion from his strange inner explosion and its shock-waves. Now they were gone, but he would not permit himself to sink into that welter of approaching bullet, rain-damped torsos, *why do I want to be dead?* So he hung motionless for a moment between disturbance and diversion. He thought of following O'Banion into the parlor. He thought of sinking back into his panic, facing it, fighting it.

But he wasn't ready to fight, not yet, and he didn't want to run . . . and he couldn't stay like this. It was like not breathing. Anyone can stop breathing, but not for long.

"Mr. Halvorsen?"

Soft-footed, soft-voiced, timidly peering about her to be sure she was not intruding, Miss Schmidt came in. Halvorsen could have hugged her. "Come in, come in!" he cried warmly.

The half-alive smile brightened like fanned embers at his tone. "Good afternoon, Mr. Halvorsen. I was looking, that is, wondering, you know, if Mr. Bittelman was back yet, and I thought perhaps that . . ." She wet her lips and apparently thought it was worth another try. "I wanted to see him about—I mean to say, ask him if he—about something." She exhaled, took a breath, and would surely have come out with more of the same, but Halvorsen broke in.

"No, not yet. Sure picked a miserable day for a joy-ride."

"It doesn't seem to matter to the Bittelmans. Every fourth week, like clockwork." She suddenly uttered a soft little bleat of a laugh. "I'm sure I don't mean clockwork, Mr. Halvorsen, I mean, four weeks."

He laughed politely, for her sake. "I know what you mean." He saw her drop her eyes to her kneading hands, divined that her next movement would be toward the door. He felt he couldn't bear that, not just now. "How about—uh—a cup of tea or something. Sandwich. I was just going to—" He rose.

She went pink and smiled again. "Why, I—"

There was a short, sibilant sound in the door-

way, a sniff, a small snort of anger. Mary Haunt stood there glowering. Miss Schmidt said, faintly, "No, no thank you, I'd better, I mean, just go and . . . I only wanted to see if Mr. Bittelman was—" She faded out altogether and tiptoed apologetically to the door. Mary Haunt swung her shoulders but did not move her feet. Miss Schmidt slid out and escaped past her.

Halvorsen found himself standing, half angry, half foolish. His own last words echoed in his mind: "Sandwich. I was just going to—" and he let them push him to the other end of the kitchen. He was furious, but why? Nothing had happened; a lot had happened. He would have liked to rear back on his hind legs and blast her for persecuting a little defenseless rabbit like Miss Schmidt; yet what had she actually done? Couldn't she say with absolute truth, "Why, I never said a word to her!"? He felt ineffectual, unmanned; and the picture of the flimsy gun flickered inside his eyelids and shocked him. He trembled, pulled himself together, painfully aware of the bright angry eyes watching his back from the doorway. He fumbled into the breadbox and took out half a loaf of Bitty's magnificent home-baked bread. He took down the breadboard and got a knife from the drawer, and began to saw. Behind him he heard a sharp slap as Mary Haunt tossed her magazine on the table beside the coffeepot, and then he was conscious of her at his elbow. If she had said one word, she would have faced a blaze of anger out of all proportion to anything that had happened. But she didn't, and didn't: she simply stood there and watched him. He finished cut-

ting the first slice, started on the second. He almost swung to face her but checked the motion, whereupon the knife bit into the first joint of his thumb. He closed his eyes, finished cutting the bread, and turned away to the refrigerator. He opened it and then bent over the shelves, holding his cut thumb in his other hand.

"What do you think you're doing?" asked the girl.

"What's it look like?" he growled. His cut suddenly began to hurt.

"I couldn't say," said Mary Haunt. She stepped to the breadboard, picked up the knife and with it whisked the bread he had cut into the sink.

"Hey!"

"You better push that cut up against the freezer coils for a second," she said with composure. She put a hand on the loaf and with one sweep straightened its hacked end. "Sit down," she said as he filled his lungs to roar at her. "If there's anything I hate it's to see someone clumsy paddling around in food." One, two, three, four even slices fell to the board as she spoke. And again she interrupted him just as he was forming a wounded-bear bellow, "You want a sandwich or not? Just sit down over there and stay out from underfoot."

Slackjawed, he watched her. Was she doing him a kindness? Mary Haunt doing someone a *kindness*?

He found himself obeying her, pressing his cut against the freezer coils. It felt good. He withdrew his hand just as she came toward the

refrigerator, and dodged out of her way. He backed to the table, sat down, and watched her.

She was something to watch. The pale, over-manicured hands flew. She set out mayonnaise, cream cheese, a platter of cold-cuts, parsley, radishes. With almost a single motion she put a small frying pan and a butter-melter on the stove and lit the fire under them. Into the frying pan went a couple of strips of bacon; into the other, two tablespoons of water and half the fluid from a jar of capers. She added spices, "by ear"—a shake, a pinch: poultry seasoning, oregano, garlic salt. The tiny pan began to hiss, and suddenly the kitchen smelt like the delivery entrance to paradise. She snatched it off, scraped the contents into a bowl, added cream cheese and mayonnaise, and thrust it under the electric mixer. She turned the bacon, shoved two of the bread slices into the toaster, and busied herself with a paring knife and the radishes.

Halvorsen shook his head unbelievingly and muttered an exclamation. The girl threw him a look of such intense scorn that he dropped his eyes. He found them resting on her magazine. It was called *Family Day* and was a homemaking publication from a chain supermarket—in no way a movie magazine.

Out of the frying pan came the bacon, crackling. She drained it on a paper towel and crumbled it into the bowl where the mixer was working. As if some kitchen choreographer was directing the work, the toast popped up as she reached out her hand for it. She dropped in the other two slices and went back to her alchemy with the radishes. In a moment she turned off

the mixer and spread the contents of the bowl on the toast. On this she laid cold-cuts, narrow strips of various kinds, deftly weaving them so they formed a beautiful basket pattern. As she finished the first two, the second pair popped out of the toaster; it was a continuous thing, the way she did all the different things she did; it was like music or a landscape flowing by a train window.

She did something swift with the knife, and set the results out on two plates: bite-sized sandwiches arranged like a star, and in the center what looked like a tiny bouquet of rosebuds—the radishes, prepared with curled petals and nested in a neat bed of parsley, its stems all drawn together by one clever half-hitch in one of them. The whole amazing performance had taken perhaps six minutes. "You can make your own coffee," she snapped.

He came over and picked up one of the plates. "Why, this is—is—well, *thanks*!" He looked at her and smiled. "Come on, let's sit down."

"With *you*?" She stalked to the table, carrying the other plate, and scooped up the magazine as if it were a guilty secret. She went to the door. "You can clean up," she said, "and if you ever tell anyone about this I'll snatch you baldheaded."

Staring after her, stunned, he absently picked up one of the sandwiches and bit into it, and for a moment forgot even his amazement, it was so delicious. He sat down slowly, and for the first time since he had started comparing violins with guitars in the pawn-shop, he gave himself up completely to his senses and forgot his

troubles. He ate the sandwiches slowly and appreciatively and let them own him.

EXCERPT FROM FIELD EXPEDITION [NOTE-BOOK]: So [weary-irritated] [I] can barely [write]. As if this kind of research wasn't arduous enough at the best of times, which this is not, with the best of equipment, which [we] lack, [I] am plagued by a [partner-teammate] with insuperable enthusiasm and a quality [I] can only describe as headlong stubbornness. [Smith] means well, of course, but the universe is full of well-meaning [individuals] [who] have succeeded only in making [   ]s of themselves.

All during the tedious and infuriating process of re[charging] the [wadget] [Smith] argued that purely objective observation would get [us] nowhere and would take [forever]; that [we] have sufficient data now to apply stimuli to these specimens and determine once and for all if a reliable, functional condition of Synapse Beta sub Sixteen is possible to them. [I] of course objected that it is against [our] highest [ethic] to apply [force] to alien species; [Smith] then argued that it would not really be [force], but only the [magnification-amplification-increased efficiency] of that which they already possessed. [I] then pointed out that even if [we] succeed, [we] can only test the final result by means which may readily kill some or all the specimens. This [Smith] is willing to worry about only when the time comes. [I] pointed out further that in order to supply the necessary stimuli [we] shall have to re[wire] not only the [widget], but that [   ]ed,

inefficient, [stone] age excuse for a [mecha-nism], the [wadget]. [Smith] readily agreed, and while [I] went on arguing [he] began re[wiring], and [I] argued, and [he] [wired], and by the time [I]'d [made my point] [he] was practically fin-ished and [I] found [myself] holding the [light] as well.

[I] forgot to ask [Smith] what [he] planned to do if one of the specimens finds out what [we]'re up to. Kill it? Kill them all? It wouldn't [surprise] [me]. In the name of [research] [Smith] would happily [watch] [his] [elderly forebear]'s [knuckles] being [knurled].

IV

Miss Schmidt, muffled up to the pharynx in a quilted robe, bed-socked, slippered and shawled, half-dozed in her easy chair. When she heard the sounds she had waited for, she jumped up, went to her door, which was ajar, and stood a moment to listen and be sure. Then she tightened her sash, checked the hooks-and-eyes under her chin, tugged her voluminous robe downward at the hips, and pulled the shawl a little higher on her shoulders. She crossed her arms at the wrists and pressed her hands modestly against her collarbones and scurried silently past the bathroom, down the long hall to the foyer. Bitty was in the kitchen and Sam Bittelman was hanging up a damp trench coat on the hall tree.

"Mr. Bittleman—"

"Sam," he corrected jovially. "Top of the

morning to you, Miss Schmidt. It turned morning, y'know, ten minutes ago."

"Oh dear yes, I know it's late," she whispered. "And I'm terribly sorry, really I am, I wouldn't for the world trouble you. I mean, I *am* sorry, I don't want to be a nuisance. Oh *dear!*" Her perennially frightened face crinkled with her small explosion of distress.

"Now you just tell me what's troubling you, lady, and we'll get it fixed," he said warmly.

"You're very kind. Very kind. It happens there is something. I mean, something to fix. In . . . in my *room.*" She bent forward with this, as with a deep confidence.

"Well, let's go have a look. Bitty!" Miss Schmidt put a shocked hand over her lips as he raised his voice. "I'm going to fix something for the lady. Be right with you." He turned back to Miss Schmidt and made a jocular bow. "Lead on."

"We mustn't wake the . . . anybody," she reproved him, then blushed because she had. He only grinned, and followed her back to her room. She entered, opened the door as wide as it would go, and self-consciously picked up the wastepaper basket and set it to hold the door open. She looked up from this task right into Sam's twinkling eyes, and sent up a prayer that he wouldn't tease her about it. One never knew what Sam was going to say; sometimes he was beyond understanding and sometimes he was just—awful. "The window," she said. "The blind."

He looked at it. "Oh, that again. Durn things are always getting the cords frayed." The ve-

netian blind hung askew, the bottom slats almost vertical, leaving a lower corner of the
window exposed. Sam tugged at the raising-
cord. It was double; one part was jammed tight
and the other ran free. He pulled it all the way
out and ruefully exhibited the broken end.
"See? That's it, all right. Have to see if I can't
put in a new cord for you in the morning, if I
can find one."

"In the morning? But—I mean, well, Mr. uh—
Sam, what about now? That is, what am I going
to *do*?"

"Why, just don't worry your pretty little head
about it! Get your beauty-sleep, little lady, and
by the time you're back from school tomorrow
I'll have it—"

"You don't understand," she wailed softly, "I
can't go to bed with it like that. That's why I
waited up for you. I've tried everything. The
drapes won't go across it and there's nothing to
hang a towel to and the chair-back isn't high
enough to cover it and—and—oh, *dear!*"

"Oh-h-h."

Struck by something in his single, slow syllable, she looked sharply at him. There was
something—what was it? like a hum in the
room. But it wasn't a sound. He hadn't changed
. . . and yet there was something in his eyes she
had never seen before. She had never seen it in
anyone's eyes. About Sam Bittelman there had
always been a leisurely strength, and it was
there now but easier, stronger, more comforting than ever. To her, with her multiple indeci-
sions, unsurenesses, his friendly certitude was
more wondrous than a halo might have been.

He said, "Just what bothers you about the window?"

Her usual self moved quite clearly to indicate, indignantly, that part of the window was uncovered and surely that spoke for itself; yet her usual self was unaccountably silent, and she gave him his answer: "Somebody might look *in*!"

"You know what's outside that window?"

"Wh—Oh. Oh, the back of the garage."

"So nobody's going to see in. Well now, suppose there was no garage, and you turned out your lights. Could anybody see in?"

"N-no . . ."

"But it still bothers you."

"Yes, of course it does." She looked at the triangle of exposed glass, black with night outside, and shuddered. He leaned against the doorpost and scratched his head. "Let me ask you something," he said, as if her permission might make a difference. "S'pose we took away the garage, and you forgot and left your light on, *and* somebody saw you?"

She squeaked.

"Really bothers you, don't it?" He laughed easily, and instead of infuriating her, the sound flooded her with comfort. "What exactly is bothersome about that, aside from the fact that it's bothersome?"

"Why . . . why," she said breathlessly, "I know what *I'd* think of a hussy that would parade around that way with the lights on and—"

"I didn't say parade. Nor 'prance,' either, which is the other word people use, I don't know why. So what really bothers you is what

some peepin' Tom might think, hm? Now, Miss Schmidt, is that really anything to worry about? What do you care what he thinks you are? Don't you know what you are?" He paused, but she had nothing to say. "You ever sleep naked?"

She gasped, and, round-eyed, shook her head.

"Why not?" he demanded.

"Why I—I—" She had to answer him; she had to. Fear rose like a thin column of smoke within her, and then a swift glance at his open, friendly face dispelled it completely. It was extraordinary, uncomfortable, exhilarating, disturbing, exciting all at once. He compelled her and comforted her at the same time.

She found her voice and answered him. "I just couldn't sleep . . . like that. Suppose there was a fire?"

"Who said that?" he snapped.

"I beg your—"

"Who said 'suppose there's a fire?' Who told you that?"

"Why, I suppose it—yes, it was my mother."

"Not your idea then. Figured as much. 'Thou shalt not kill.' Do you believe that?"

"Of course!"

"You do. How old were you when you learned that?"

"I don't—know. All children—"

"Children seven, eight, nine? All right. How old were you when you were taught not to unpin your diapers? Not to let anyone *see* you?"

She did not answer but the answer was there.

"Wouldn't you say you'd learned 'thou shalt not expose thy body' earlier, better, more down-deep than 'thou shalt not kill'?"

"I—yes."

"Do you realize it's a deeper commandment with you than any of the Ten? And aside from right-'n-wrong, isn't it deeper than the deepest, strongest one of all—save thyself? Can't you see yourself dying under a bush rather than walk naked out on the road and flag a car? 'Suppose there's a fire?' Can't you see yourself burn to death rather'n jump out a window without your bathrobe?"

She didn't answer except from her round eyes and her whole heart.

"Does that make any *sense*, to believe a thing like that?"

"I don't know," she whispered. "I—have to think."

Surprisingly, he said, "Retroactive." He pointed to the window. "What can we do about that?" he asked.

Absently she glanced at it. "Never mind it tonight, Mr. Bittelman."

"Sam. Okay. Goodnight, little lady."

She felt herself, abruptly, tottering on the edge of a bottomless pit. He had walked in here and disoriented her, ripped into shreds a whole idea-matrix which had rested undisturbed in the foundations of her thinking, like a cornerstone. Just at this startled second she had not made the admission, but she would have to admit to herself soon that she must think "retroactive," as he had put it, and that when she did she would find that the clothes convention was not the only one she would have to reappraise. The inescapable, horizonless, unfamiliar task loomed over her like a black cloud—her only

comfort, her only handhold was Sam Bittelman, and he was leaving. "No!" she cried. "No!
No! No!"

He turned back, smiling, and that magic happened again, his sureness and ease. She stood
gasping as if she had run up a hill.

"It's all right, little lady."

"Why did you tell me all this? Why?" she
asked pathetically.

"You know something? I didn't tell you a
thing," he said. "I just asked questions. They
were all questions you could've asked yourself.
And what's got you scared is answers—answers
that came from here—" He put a gentle knuckle
against her damp forehead. "—and not from
me. You've lived with it all quite a while; you
got nothing to fear from it now." And before
she could answer he had waved one capable
hand, winked, and was gone.

For a long time she stood there, trembling
and afraid to think. At last she let her open eyes
see again, and although they saw nothing but
the open door, it was as if some of Sam's comfort slipped in with vision. She turned around,
and around again, taking in the whole room and
reaping comfort and more comfort from the
walls, as if Sam had hung it for her to gather
like ripe berries. She put it all in the new empty
place within her, not to fill, but at least to be
there and to live with until she could get more.
Suddenly her gaze met the silly little wastebas-
ket sitting against the door, holding it open, and
to her utter astonishment she laughed at it. She
picked it up, shook her head at it as if it had
been a ridiculous puppy which had been eating

her talcum powder; she even spanked it lightly, once, and put it down, and closed the door. She got into bed and put out the light without even looking at the window.

V

"Aw, you shouldn't!" cried Bitty with a joyous sort of chagrin as she pushed open Sue Martin's door. "Here I've got all your fresh linen and you've went and made the bed!"

Sue Martin, sleep-tousled and lovely in a dark negligee, rose from the writing desk. "I'm sorry, Bitty. I forgot it was Thursday."

"Well Thursday it is," the older woman scolded, "and now I'll have to do it up all over again. Young lady, I've told and *told* you I'll take care of the room."

"You have plenty to do," Sue smiled. "Here, I'll help. What's Robin up to?"

Together they took down the spread, the light blanket, then the sheets from the big double bed. "Kidnaped by that young idiot O'Banion again. He's driving out to the new project over Huttonville way and thought Robin might want to see the bulldozers."

"Robin loves bulldozers. He's not an idiot."

"He's an idiot," said Bitty gruffly, apparently needing no translation of the two parts of Sue's statement. "Time this was turned, since we're both here," she said, swatting the mattress.

"All right," Sue Martin loosely folded the spread and blanket and carried them to the chest. "Robin just loves him."

"So do you."

Sue's eyes widened. She shot a look at the other woman, but Bitty's back was turned as she bent over the bed. When she spoke, her voice was perfectly controlled. "Yes, for some time." She went to stand beside Bitty and they laid hold of the mattress straps. "Ready?" Together they heaved and the mattress rose up, teetered for a moment on edge, and fell back the other way. They pulled it straight.

"Well, what are you doing about it?" Bitty demanded.

Sue found her eyes captured by Bitty's for a strange moment. She saw herself, in a flash of analog, walking purposefully away, from some tired, dark place toward something she wanted; and as she walked there appeared humming softly behind her, around her, something like a moving wall. She had a deep certainty that she could not stop nor turn aside; but that as long as she kept moving at the same speed, in the same direction, the moving wall could not affect her. She—and it—were moving toward what she wanted, just as fast as she cared to go. While this was the case, she was not being restrained or compelled, helped nor hindered. So she would not fear this thing, fight it or even question it. It could not possibly change anything. In effect, irresistible as it might be, it need not and therefore did not exist for her. Here and now, some inexplicable something had happened to make it impossible not to answer Bitty's questions—and this compulsion was of no moment at all for her as long as Bitty asked questions she wanted to answer. "What are you doing about it?" was such a question.

"Everything I should do," said Sue Martin. "Nothing at all."

Bitty grunted noncommittally. She took a folded sheet from the top of the highboy and shook it out across the bed. Sue Martin went round to the other side and caught it. She said, "He has to know why, that's all, and he can't do anything or say anything until he does know."

"Why what?" Bitty asked bluntly.

"Why he loves me."

"Oh—you know that, do you?"

This was one question, compulsion or no, that Sue Martin did not bother to answer. It was on the order of "Is this really a bed?" or "Is it Thursday?" So Bitty asked another: "And you're just waiting, like a little edelweiss on an Alp, for him to climb the mountain and pick you?"

"Waiting?" Sue repeated, puzzled.

"You're not doing anything about it, are you?"

"I'm being myself," said Sue Martin. "I'm living my life. What I have to give him—anyone who's *right* for me—is all I am, all I do for the rest of my life. As long as he wants something more, or something different, nothing can happen." She closed her eyes for a moment. "No, I'm not waiting, exactly. Put it this way: I know how to be content with what I am and what I'm doing. Either Tony will knock down that barrier he's built, or he won't. Either way I know what's going to happen, and it's good."

"That wall—why don't you take a pickax and beat it down?"

She flashed the older woman a smile, "He'd de-

fend it. Men get very fond of the things they defend, especially when they find themselves defending something stupid."

Bitty shook out the second sheet. "And don't you have any of his kind of trouble—wondering *why* you love him?"

Sue Martin laughed. "Wouldn't we live in a funny world if we had to understand everything that was real, or it wouldn't exist? It's always good to know *why*. It isn't always necessary. Tony'll find that out one day." She sobered. "Or he won't. Hand me a pillowslip."

They finished their task in silence. Bitty bundled up the old linen and trudged out. Sue Martin stood looking after her. "I hope she wasn't disappointed," she murmured, and, "I don't think so . . . and what did I mean by that?"

VI

One morning Mary Haunt opened her eyes and refused to believe them. For a moment she lay still looking at the window numbly; there was something wrong with it, and a wrong feeling about the whole room. Then she identified it: there was sunlight streaming in and down through the venetian blind where no sunlight should be at her rising time. She snatched her watch off the night table and squinted at it, and moaned. She reared up in bed and peered at the alarm clock, then turned and punched furiously at the pillow. She bounded out of bed, struggled into her yellow robe, and flew out of the room with her bare feet slapping angrily down the long corridor. Sam Bittelman was sitting at the

kitchen table peering at the morning paper over the tops of his black rimmed reading-glasses. Bitty was at the sink. "What 'm I, the forgotten man or something?" Mary Haunt demanded harshly.

Sam put down his paper and only then began to remove his gaze from it. "M-m-m? Oh, good morning, gal." Bitty went on with her business.

"Good *nothing*! Don't you know what time it is?"

"Sure do."

"What's the big fat idea leaving me to sleep like this? You know I got to get to work in the morning."

"Who called you four times?" said Bitty without turning around or raising her voice. "Who went in and shook you, and got told *get out of my room* for it?"

Mary Haunt poised between pace and pace, between syllables. Now that Bitty mentioned it, she *did* half-remember a vague hammering somewhere, a hand on her shoulder . . . but that was a dream, or the middle of the night or—or had she really chased the old lady out? "*Arrgh*," she growled disgustedly. She stamped out into the foyer and snatched up the phone. She dialed. "Get me Muller," she snapped at the voice that answered.

"Muller," said the phone.

"Mary Haunt here. I'm sick today. I'm not coming in."

"So with this phone call," said the telephone, "I'll notice."

"Why you lousy Heine, without me you couldn't run a yo-yo, let alone a radio station!"

she shouted, but she had hung up before she started to shout.

She padded back into the kitchen and sat down at the table. "Got coffee?"

Bitty, still with her back turned, nodded in the appropriate direction and said, "On the stove," but Sam folded his paper and got up. He went to the stove, touched the pot briefly with the back of his hand, picking up a cup and saucer on the way. "You'll want milk."

"You know better than that," she said, arching her lean body. While she poured herself a cup, Sam sat down at the other end of the table. He leaned his weight on his elbows, his forearms and worn hands flat on the table. Something like the almost-silent whisper from a high-speed fan made her look up. "What are you looking at?"

He didn't answer her question. "Why do you claim to be twenty-two?" he asked instead, and quick as the rebound of billiard ball from cue ball, propelled by hostility, inclusive as buckshot, her reply jetted up: "*What's it to you?*" But it never reached her lips; instead she said "I have to," and then sat there astounded. Once she had worn out a favored phonograph record, knew every note, every beat of it, and she had replaced it; and for once the record company had made a mistake and the record was not what the label said it was. The first half-second of that new record was like this, a moment of expectation and stunned disbelief. This was even more immediate and personal, however; it was like mounting ten steps in the dark and finding, shockingly, that there were only nine in

the flight. From this moment until she left the kitchen, she was internally numb and frightened, yet fascinated, as her mind formed one set of words and others came out.

"You have to," asked Sam mildly, "the way you have to be in the movies? You just *have* to?"

The snarl, *have I kept it a secret?* came out, "It's what I want."

"Is it?"

There didn't seem to be any answer to that, on any level. She waited, tense.

"What you're doing—the job at the radio station—living here in this town instead of someplace else—all of it; is what you're doing the best way to get what you want?"

Why else would I put up with it all—the town, the people—you? But she said, "I think so." Then she said, "I've thought so."

"Why don't you talk to young Halvorsen? He might be able to find something you'd do even better'n going to Hollywood."

"I don't *want* to find anything better!" This time there was no confusion.

From the other end of the room, Bitty asked, "Were you always so all-fired pretty, Mary Haunt? Even when you were a little girl?"

"Everyone always said so."

"Ever wish you weren't?"

Are you out of your mind? "I . . . don't think so," she whispered.

Gently, Sam asked her, "Did they throw you out, gal? Make you leave home?"

Defiantly, defensively, *They treated me like a little princess at home, like a piece of fine glass-*

ware. They carried my books and felt good all day if I smiled. They did what I wanted, what they thought I wanted, at home or in town. They acted as if I was too good to walk that ground, breathe that air, they jumped at the chance to take advantage of being at the same place at the same time; they did everything for me they could think of doing, as if they had to hurry or I'd be gone. Throw me out? Why, you old fool! "I left home my own self," she said. "Because I had to, like—" But here words failed her, and she determined not to cry, and she determined not to cry, and she cried.

"Better drink your coffee."

She did, and then she wanted something to eat with it, but couldn't bear to sit with these people any longer. She sniffed angrily. "I don't know what's the matter with me," she said. "I never overslept before."

"Long as you know what you want," said Sam, and whether that was the stupid, non-sequitur remark of a doddering dotard, or something quite diffcrent, she did not know. "Well," she said, rising abruptly; and then felt foolish because there was nothing else to say. She escaped back to her room and to bed, and huddled there most of the day dully regarding the two coddled ends of her life, pampering in the past and pampering in the future, while trying to ignore today with its empty stomach and its buzzing head.

VII

During Prohibition it had been a restaurant, in that category which is better than just "nice" but not as good as "exclusive"; the town was too small then to have anything exclusive. Now it was a bar as well, and although there was imitation Carrara on some walls, and a good deal of cove-lighting, the balcony had never been altered and still boasted the turned-spoke railing all the way around, looking like a picket fence that had gone to heaven. There was a little service bar up there, and a man could stay all evening watching what went on down below without being seen. This was what Tony O'Banion was doing, and he was doing it because he had felt like a drink and had never been to the club before, and he wanted to see what kind of place it was and what Sue Martin did there; and every one of these reasons were superficial—if he preceded them with "Why," he felt lost. Within him were the things he believed, about the right sort of people, about background, breeding and blood. Around him was this place, as real as the things he believed in. *Why* he was here, why he wanted a drink just now, why he wanted to see the place and what happened in it—this was a bridge between one reality and the other, and a misty, maddening, nebulous bridge it was. He drank, and waited to see her emerge from the small door by the bandstand, and when she did he watched her move to the piano and help the pianist, a disheveled young man, stack and restack and shuffle his music, and he drank. He drank, and watched her go to

the cashier and spend a time over a ledger and a pile of checks. She disappeared through the swinging doors into the kitchen, and he drank; he drank and she came out talking to a glossy man in a tuxedo, and he winced when they laughed.

At length the lights dimmed and the glossy man introduced her and she sang in a full, pleasant voice something about a boy next door, and someone else played an accordion which was the barest shade out of tune with the piano. Then the piano had a solo, and the man sang the last chorus, after which the lights came up again and he asked the folks to stick around for the main show at ten sharp. Then the accordion and the piano began to make dance music. It was all unremarkable, and Tony didn't know why he stayed. He stayed, though: "Waiter! Do it again."

"Do it twice."

Tony spun around. "Time someone else bought, hm?" said Sam Bittelman. He sat down.

"Sam! Well, sit down. Oh, you *are*." Tony laughed embarrassedly. His tongue was thick and he was immeasurably glad to see the old man. He was going to wonder why until he remembered that he'd sworn off wondering why just now. He was going to ask what Sam was doing there and then decided Sam would only ask him the same, and it was a question he didn't want to fool with just now. Yes he did.

"I'm down here slumming in the fleshpots and watching the lower orders cavorting and carousing," he blurted, making an immense effort

to be funny. He wasn't funny. He sounded like a little snob, and a tight little snob at that.

Sam regarded him gravely, not disapproving, not approving. "Sue Martin know you're here?"

"No."

"Good."

The waiter came just in time; Sam's single syllable had given him a hard hurt; but for all the pain, it was an impersonal thing, like getting hit by a golfer on his backswing. When the waiter had gone Sam asked quietly, "Why don't you marry the girl?"

"What're ya—kidding?"

Sam shook his head. O'Banion looked into his eyes and away, then down at Sue Martin where she leaned against the piano, leafing through some music, *Why don't you marry the girl?* "You mean if she'd have me?" It was not the way he felt, but it was something to say. He glanced at Sam's face, which was still waiting for a real answer. All right then. "It wouldn't be right."

" 'Right'?" Sam repeated.

O'Banion nipped his thick tongue in the hope it might wake his brains up. The rightness of it . . . vividly he recalled his Mother's words on the subject: "Aside from the amount of trouble you'll save yourself, Anthony, you must remember that it's not only your right, it's your *duty* not to marry beneath your class. Fine hounds, fine horses, fine humans, my dear; it's breeding that matters." That was all very well, but how to say it to the kind old man, himself obviously a manual worker all his life? O'Banion was not a cruel man, and he was well aware that coarse origins did not always mean dull sensibilities.

Actually, some of these people were very sensitive. So he made a genuinely noble try at simultaneous truth and kindness: "I've always felt it's wiser to form relationships like that with—uh—people of one's own kind."

"You mean, people with as much money as you got?"

"No!" O'Banion was genuinely shocked. "That's no longer a standard to go by, and it probably never was, not by itself." He laughed ruefully and added, "Besides, there hasn't been any money in my family since I can remember. Not since 1929."

"Then what's your kind of people?"

How? How? "It's . . . a way of life," he said at length. That pleased him. "A way of life," he repeated, and took a drink. He hoped Sam wouldn't pursue the subject any further. Why examine something when you're content with it the way it is?

"Why are you here anyway, boy?" Sam asked. "I mean, in this town instead of in the city, or New York or some place?"

"I'm good for a junior partnership in another year or so. Then I can transfer as a junior partner to a big firm. If I'd gone straight to the city it would take me twice as long to get up there."

Sam nodded. "Pretty cute. Why the law? I always figured lawyer's work was pretty tough and pretty dusty for a young man."

His Mother had said, "Of course the law field's being invaded by all sorts of riffraff now—but what isn't? However, it's still possible for a gentleman to do a gentleman's part in law." Well, that wouldn't do. He'd have to go

deeper. He averted his eyes from old Sam's casual penetration and said, "Tough, yes. But there's something about law work . . ." He wondered if the old man would follow this. "Look, Sam, did it ever occur to you that the law is the biggest thing ever built? It's bigger'n bridges, bigger'n buildings—because they're all built *on* it. A lawyer's a part of the law, and the law is part of everything else—everything we own, the way we run governments, everything we make and carry and use. Ever think of that?"

"Can't say I did," said Sam. "Tell me something—the law, is it finished?"

"Finished?"

"What I mean, this rock everything's built on, how solid is it? Is it going to change much? Didn't it change a whole lot to get the way it is?"

"Well, sure! Everything changes a lot while it's growing up."

"Ah. It's grown up."

"Don't you think it has?" O'Banion asked with sudden truculence.

Sam grinned easily. "Shucks, boy, I don't think. I just ask questions. You were saying about 'your sort of people': you think you-all *belong* in the law?"

"Yes!" said O'Banion, and saw immediately that Sam would not be satisfied with so little. "We do in this sense," he said earnestly. "All through the ages men have worked and built and—and owned. And among them there rose a few who were born and bred and trained to—to—" He took another drink, but it and the preceding liquor seemed not to be helping him. He

wanted to say *to rule* and he wanted to say *to own*, but he had wit enough about him to recognize that Sam would misunderstand. So he tried again. "Born and bred to—live that—uh—way of life I mentioned before. It's to the interest of those few people to invest their lives in things as they are, to keep them that way; in other words, to work for and uphold the law." He leaned back with a flourish that somehow wasn't as eloquent as he had hoped and very nearly upset his glass to boot.

"Don't the law contradict itself once in a while?"

"Naturally!" O'Banion's crystallizing concept of the nobility of his work was beginning to intoxicate him more than anything else. "But the very nature of our courts is a process of refinement, constant purification." He leaned forward excitedly. "Look, laws are dreams, when they're first thought of—inspirations! There's something . . . uh . . . holy about that, something beyond the world of men. And that's why when the world of men comes into contact with it, the wording of the inspiration has to be redone in the books, or interpreted in the courtroom. That's what we mean by 'precedents'—that's what the big dusty books are for, to create and maintain consistency under the law."

"What about justice?" murmured Sam, and then quickly, as if he hadn't meant to change the subject, "That's not what I meant by contradictin', counsellor. I mean all laws that all men have dreamed up and lived by and got theirselves killed over. Tell me something, counsellor, is there even

one single law so right for men that it shows up in every country that is or was?"

O'Banion made a startled sound, as half a dozen excellent examples flashed into his mind at once, collided, and, under the first examination, faded away.

"Because," said Sam in a voice which was friendly and almost apologetic, "if there ain't such a law, you might say every set of laws ever dreamed up, even the sets that were bigger and older and lasted longer than the one you practice, even any set you can imagine for the future— they're all goin' to contradict one another some way or other. So, who's really to say whose set of laws are right—or fit to build anything on, or breed up a handful of folks fit to run it?"

O'Banion stared at his glass without touching it. For an awful moment he was totally disoriented; a churning pit yawned under his feet and he must surely topple into it. He thought wildly, you can't leave me here, old man! You'd better say something else, and fast, or I . . . or I . . .

There was a sort of pressure in his ears, like sound too high-pitched for humans. Sam said softly, "You really think Sue Martin ain't good enough for you?"

"I didn't say that, I didn't say that!" O'Banion blurted, hoarse with indignation, and fright, and relief as well. He shuddered back and away from the lip of this personal precipice and looked redly at the composed old face. "I said different, too different, that's all. I'm thinking of her as well as—"

For once Sam bluntly interrupted, as if he

had no patience with what O'Banion was saying. "What's different?"

"Background, I told you. Don't you know
what that is?"

"You mean the closer a girl's background is
to yours, the better chance you'd have bein'
happy the rest of your life?"

"Isn't it obvious?" The perfect example popped
into his mind, and he speared a finger out and
downward toward the piano. "Did you hear what
she was singing just before you got here? 'The
boy next door.' Don't you understand what that
really means, why that song, that idea, hits home
to so many people? Everybody understands that;
it's the appeal of what's familiar, close by—the
similar background I'm talking about!"

"You have to shout?" chuckled Sam. Sober-
ing, he said, "Well, counsellor, if you're goin' to
think consistently, like you said, couldn't you
dream up a background even more sim'lar than
your next-door neighbor?"

O'Banion stared at him blankly, and old Sam
Bittelman asked, "Are you an only child, counsellor?"

O'Banion closed his eyes and saw the precipice
there waiting; he snapped them open in sheer self-
defense. His hands hurt and he looked down, and
slowly released them from the edge of the table.
He whispered, "What are you trying to tell me?"

His bland face the very portrait of candor, Sam
said, "Shucks, son, I couldn't tell you a thing, not
a blessed thing. Why, I don't know anything you
don't know to tell you! I ain't asked you a single
question you couldn't've asked yourself, and the
answers were all yours, not mine. Hey . . ." he

breathed, "you better come along home. You wouldn't want Miz Martin to see you looking the way you do right now."

Numbly, Anthony Dunglass O'Banion followed him out.

VIII

It was hot, so hot that apparently even Bitty felt it, and after supper went to sit on the verandah. It was very late when at last she came in to do the dishes, but she went ahead without hurrying, doing her usual steady, thorough job. Sam had gone to bed, Mary Haunt was sulking in her room after yet another of those brief, violent brushes with Miss Schmidt. O'Banion was crouching sweatily over some law-books in the parlor, and Halvorsen—

Halvorsen was standing behind her, just inside the kitchen. On his face was a mixture of expressions far too complicated to analyze, but simple in sum—a sort of anxious wistfulness. In his hands was a paper sack, the mouth of which he held as if it were full of tarantulas. His stance was peculiar, strained and off-balance, one foot advanced, his shoulders askew; his resolution had equated with his diffidence and immobilized him, and there he stayed like a bee in amber.

Bitty did not turn. She went right on working steadily, her back to him, until she finished the pot she was scouring. Still without turning, she reached for another and said, "Well, come on in, Philip."

Halvorsen literally sagged as her flat, matter-

of-fact voice reached him, shattering with its exterior touch his interior deadlock. He grinned, or just bared his teeth, and approached her. "You *do* have eyes in the back of your head."

"Nup." She rapped once with her knuckle on the windowpane over the sink. Night had turned it to black glass. Halvorsen watched the little cone of suds her hand had left, then refocused his eyes on the image in the glass—vivid, the kitchen and everything in it. Hoarsely, he said, "I'm disappointed."

"I don't keeps things I don't need," she said bluntly, as if they'd been talking about apple-corers. "What's on your mind? Hungry?"

"No." He looked down at his hands, tightened them still more on the bag. "No," he said again, "I have, I wanted . . ." He noticed that she had stopped working and was standing still, inhumanly still, with her hands in the dishwater and her eyes on the window-pane. "Turn around, Bitty."

When she would not, he supported the bottom of the paper bag with one hand and with the other scrabbled it open. He put his hands down inside it. "Please," he tried to say, but it was only a hiss.

She calmly shook water off her hands, wiped them on a paper towel. When she turned around her face was eloquent—as always, and only because it always was. Its lines were eloquent, and the shape of her penetrating eyes, and the light in them. As a photograph or a painting such a face is eloquent. It is a frightening thing to look into one and realize for the first time that behind it nothing need be moving. Behind the lines

of wisdom and experience and the curved spoor of laughter, something utterly immobile could be waiting. Only waiting.

Halvorsen said, "I think all the time." He wet his lips. "I never stop thinking, I don't know how. It's . . . there's something wrong."

Flatly, "What's wrong?"

"You, Sam," said Halvorsen with difficulty. He looked down at the bag over his hand. She did not. "I've had the . . . feeling . . . for a long time now. I didn't know what it was. Just something wrong. So I talked to O'Banion. Miss Schmidt too. Just, you know, talk." He swallowed. "I found out. What's wrong, I mean. It's the way you and Sam talk to us, all of us." He gestured with the paper bag. *"You never say anything!* You only ask questions!"

"Is that all?" asked Bitty good-humoredly.

"No," he said, his eyes fixed on hers. He stepped back a pace.

"Aren't you afraid that paper bag'll spoil your aim, Philip?"

He shook his head. His face turned the color of putty.

"You didn't go out and buy a gun just for me, did you?"

"You see?" he breathed. "Questions. You see?"

"You already had it, didn't you, Philip? Bought it for something else?"

"Stay away from me," he whispered, but she had not moved. He said, "Who are you? What are you after?"

"Philip," she said gently—and now she smiled. "Philip—*why do you want to be dead?*"

PART TWO

SPECIAL ENTRY IN FIELD EXPEDITION [NOTEBOOK]: Since it is now [my] intention to prefer charges against [my] [partner-teammate] [Smith] and to use these [notes] as a formal [document] in the matter, [I] shall now summarize in detail the particulars of the case: [We] have been on Earth for [expression of time-units] on a field expedition to determine whether or not the dominant species here possesses the Synapse known to our [catalog] as Beta sub Sixteen, the master [computer] [at home] having concluded that without the Synapse, this Earth culture must become extinct. Needless to [say] [we] are here to observe and not to interfere; to add to the [memory-banks] of the master [computer] only, it being a matter of no significance otherwise.

On arrival [we] set up the usual [detectors], expecting to get our information in a [expression of very short time-unit] or so; but to our [great astonishment] the readings on the [kickshaw], the [gimmick] and our high-sensitivity [snivvy] were mixed; it appears that this culture possessed the Synapse but did not use it. [!!!]

[We] therefore decided to conduct a [micro-

cosmic] observation on each of the specimens in a small group, under [laboratory] conditions, to discover to what extent the Synapse exists in them, and under what circumstances it might become functional. We have set up for this purpose [the analog of] a [   ], or [residence], called, in Terrestrial terms, *small town boarding house,* and have attracted to it:

PHILIP HALVORSEN, a young vocational guidance expert, who has a ceaselessly active analytical mind, and a kind of instinct for illogic: he knows when a person or situation is, in some way, wrong, and will not rest until he finds out why. He has recently followed his own logic to the conclusion that he wants to be dead—and he can't find out why! . . . MARY HAUNT, a beautiful girl who claims to be twenty-two [and lies], and who wants to be a movie star with an ambition transcending all reason. She is employed in a very minor capacity at the local radio station, and is always angry at everyone. . . . ANTHONY DUNGLASS O'BANION, a young lawyer, deeply convinced that his family background, "breeding," "culture" and occupation set him apart from everyone else in town; he is desperately fighting a growing conviction that he is in love with . . . SUE MARTIN, young widowed night-club hostess [whom O'Banion's Mother, if she were here, would certainly refer to as a "woman of that sort"]. Sue Martin, a woman of unusual equilibrium, loves O'Banion but will not submit herself to his snobbery and therefore keeps her feelings very much to herself. . . . Her young son ROBIN who is three, and is friends with everyone everywhere in-

cluding his invisible, "imaginary" playmates Boff and Googie. Robin's special friend is the lawyer O'Banion; they get along very well indeed. . . . Finally, MISS SCHMIDT, the high-school librarian, who is a soft-voiced, timid little rabbit of a woman, afraid of the world and abjectly obedient to propriety.

The retired couple who run the boarding house are SAM and BITTY BITTELMAN, wise, relaxed, helpful, observant. They are available always except for one day a month when they go out "for a ride."

That, in Terrestrial terms, is [our] laboratory setup. [We] installed a [widget] and [rigged-up] a [wadget] as complementary [observation-and-control] even though it meant using a [miserable] [inefficient] [old-fashioned] power supply on the [wadget], which has to be re[charged] every [equivalent of Earth month]. Everything proceeded satisfactorily until [Smith], plagued by what [I] can only, in the most cosmic breadth of generosity, call an excess of enthusiasm, insisted that [we] speed up our research by stimulating the Synapse in these specimens. In spite of [my] warnings and [my] caution, [he] [bulled] ahead giving [me] no choice but to assist [him] in re[wiring] the [machines] for this purpose. But let it be on the [record] that [I] specifically warned [him] of the dangers of revealing [our] presence here. [I] for [one] dread the idea of being responsible for the destruction of organized life. Even if only one of the specimens should detect [us], there is so much intercommunication in this small group that it would be virtually impossible to remove

or destroy one without alerting and disturbing
all. The least effect would be to negate all [four]
efforts so far; the most is something [I] cannot
[ethically] live with.

Under these [unhappy] circumstances [we]
proceeded with the stimulation; Old Sam Bittelman went to Miss Schmidt's room when she
reported her venetian blind broken and un-
able to close. She suddenly found it impossible not to answer Sam's questions, which
probed at the very roots of her timidity.
Shocked to these roots, but more thoughtful
than she had ever been in her life, before, she
went to bed forgetting the blind and thinking
about the fact that her conditioning to keep her
body covered was more deeply instilled into
her than *Thou shalt not kill*—and other, equally
unsettling concepts.

Mary Haunt overslept, for the very first time,
and went into the kitchen, furious. Sam and
Bitty were there, and suddenly the girl *had* to
answer the questions they shot at her. She escaped quickly, but spent the rest of the day in
bed, miserable and disoriented, wondering if,
after all, she did want Hollywood. . . .

Anthony O'Banion went down to the night club
where Sue Martin worked, and sat out of sight
on the balcony. Suddenly Sam Bittelman was at
the table with him, asking him deeply troubling questions about the law and why he
practiced it, about his convictions of blood and
breeding, and about his feelings for Sue Martin. Dizzied and speechless, O'Banion was led
home by kind old Sam.

Bitty found Sue Martin alone in her room one

morning, and asked her some pointed questions, all of which Sue answered with ease, quite undisturbed, quite willing. Yes, she loved O'Banion. No, she wouldn't do anything about it; that was O'Banion's problem. Sue Martin was no trouble at all to Bitty. . . .

Late one hot evening Halvorsen walked into the kitchen with a gun in his hand, saying there was something wrong, something he couldn't name . . . but *"Who are you and what do you want?"* Bitty calmly asked him why he had bought a gun: "It was for yourself, wasn't it, Philip? *Why do you want to be dead?"* [I] submit that [Smith] is guilty of carelessness and [unethical] conduct. [I] see no solution but to destroy this specimen and perhaps the others. [I] declare that this situation has arisen only because [Smith] ignored [my] clearly [stated] warning. As [I] [write], this alerted, frightened specimen stands ready to commit violence on [our] [equipment] and thereby itself. [I] hereby serve notice on [Smith] that [he] got [us] into this and [he] can [   ]ing well get [us] out.

IX

"Why do you want to be dead?"

Phil Halvorsen stood gaping at the old woman, and the gun, still shrouded in its silly paper bag, began whispering softly as he trembled. The butt fitted his hand as his hand fitted the butt; *It's holding me,* he thought hysterically, knowing clearly that his hysteria was a cloud, a cloak, a defense against that which he was not equipped to think about . . . well, maybe

not ready to think about; but how had she known?

For nearly two days he had been worrying and gnawing at this sense of wrongness about him. Back and back he would come to it, only to reach bafflement and kick it away angrily; not eating enough, hardly sleeping at all; *let me sleep first!* something wailed within him, and as he sensed it he kicked it away again: more hysteria, not letting him think. And then a word from O'Banion, a phrase from Miss Schmidt, and his own ragbag memory: The Bittelmans never said—they always asked. It was as if they could reach into a man's mind, piece together questions from the unused lumber stored there, and from it build shapes he couldn't bear to look at. *How many terrible questions have I locked away?* And has she broken the lock? He said, "Don't . . . ask me that . . . why did you ask me that?"

"Well, why ever not?"

"You're a . . . you can read my mind."

"Can I?"

"*Say* something!" he shouted. The paper bag stopped whispering. He thought she noticed it.

"Am I reading your mind," she asked reasonably, "if I see you walk in here the way you did looking like the wrath o' God, holding that thing out in front of you and shying away from it at the same time, and then tell you that if you accidentally pull the trigger you might have to die for it? Read minds? Isn't it enough to read the papers?"

Oh, he thought. . . . Oh-h. He looked at her sharply. She was quite calm, waiting, leaving it

to him. He knew, suddenly and certainly, that this woman could outthink him, outtalk him, seven ways from Sunday without turning a hair. This meant either that he was completely and embarrassingly wrong, or that her easy explanations weren't true ones ... which was the thing that had been bothering him in the first place. "Why did you say I bought the gun for something else?" he snapped.

She gave him that brief, very-warm smile. "Didn't say; I asked you, right? How could I really know?"

For one further moment he hesitated, and it came to him that if this flickering doubt about her was justified, the chances were that a gun would be as ineffective as an argument. And besides ... it was like a silent current in the room, a sort of almost-sound, or the aural pressure he could feel sometimes when a car was braking near him; but here it came out feeling like comfort.

He let the bag fall until it swung from its mouth. He twisted it closed. "Will you—I mean," he bumbled, "I don't want it."

"Now what would I do with a gun?" she asked.

"I don't know. I just don't want it around. I can throw it away. I don't want to have anything to do with it. I thought maybe you could put it away somewhere."

"You know, you'd better sit down," said Bitty. She didn't exactly push him but he had to move back to get out of her way as she approached, and when the back of his knees hit a chair he had to sit down or fall down. Bitty con-

tinued across the kitchen, opened a high cup-
board and put the bag on the topmost shelf.
"Only place in the house Robin can't climb
into."

"Robin. Oh yes," he said, seeing the possibil-
ities. "I'm sorry. I'm sorry."

"You'd better talk it out, Philip," she said in
her flat, kind way. "You're fixing to bust wide
open. I won't have you messing up my kitchen."

"There's nothing to talk about."

She paused on her way back to the sink, in a
strange hesitation like one listening. Suddenly
she turned and sat down at the table with him.
"What did you want with a gun, Philip?" she
demanded; and just as abruptly, he answered
her, as if she had hurled something at him and
it had bounced straight back into her waiting
hands, "I was thinking about killing myself."

If he thought this would elicit surprise, or an
exclamation, or any more questions, he was disappointed. She seemed only to be waiting, so he
said, with considerably more care, "I don't
know why I told you that but it came out right.
I said I was thinking about doing it. I didn't say
I was going to do it." He looked at her. Not
enough? Okay then: "I couldn't be sure exactly
what I was thinking until I bought a gun. Does
that make any sense to you?"

"Why not?"

"I don't ever know exactly what I think unless I try it out. Or get all the pieces laid out
ready to try."

"Or tell somebody?"

"I couldn't tell anybody about this."

"Did you try?"

"*Damn* it!" It was a whisper, but it emerged under frightening pressure. Then normally, "I'm sorry, Bitty, I'm real sorry. I suddenly got mad at the language, you know what I mean? You say something in words of one syllable and it comes out meaning something you never meant. I told you, 'I couldn't tell anybody about this.' That sounds as if I knew all about it and was just shy or something. So you ask me, 'Did you try?' But what I really mean was that this whole thing, everything about it, is a bunch of—of feelings, and—well, crazy ideas *that I couldn't tell anyone about.*"

Bitty's rare smile flickered. "Did you try?"

"Well I'll be. You're worse than ever," he said, this time without anger. "You *do* know what I'm thinking."

"So what were you thinking?"

He sobered immediately. "Things . . . all crazy. I think all the time, Bitty, like a radio was playing all day, all night, and I can't turn it off. Wouldn't want to; wouldn't know how to live without it. Ask me is it going to rain and off I go, thinking about rain, where it comes from, about clouds, how many different kinds there are; about air-currents and jet-streams and everything else you pick up reading those little paragraphs at the bottom of newspaper columns; about—"

"About why you bought a gun?"

"Huh? Oh . . . all right, all right, I won't ramble." He closed his eyes to hear his thoughts, and frowned at them. "Anyway, at the tail end of these run-downs is always some single thing that stops the chain—for the time. It might be

the answer to some question I asked myself, or someone asks me, or it might just be as far as the things I know will take me.

"So one day a few weeks ago I got to thinking about guns, and never mind the way I went, but what I arrived at was the idea of a gun killing me, and then just the idea of being dead. And the more I thought, the more scared I got."

After waiting what seemed to be long enough, Bitty said, "Scared."

"It wasn't kil—being dead that scared me. It was the feeling I had about it. I was glad about it. I wanted it. That's what scared me."

"Why do you want to be dead?"

"That's what I don't know." His voice fell. "Don't know, I just don't know," he mumbled. "So I couldn't get it out of my head and I couldn't make any sense out of it, and I thought the only thing I could do was to get a gun and load it and—get everything ready, to see how I felt then." He looked up at her. "That sounds real crazy, I bet."

Bitty shrugged. Either she denied the statement or it didn't matter. Halvorsen looked down again and said to his clenched hands, "I sat there in my room with the muzzle in my mouth and all the safeties off, and hooked my thumb around the trigger."

"Learn anything?"

His mouth moved but he couldn't find words to fit the movement. "Well," said Bitty sharply, "why didn't you pull it?"

"I just—" He closed his eyes in one of those long, inward-reading pauses. "—couldn't. I mean, *didn't*. I wasn't afraid, if that's what you

want to know." He glanced at her and couldn't tell what she wanted to know. "Sitting there, that way, I came to realize that this wasn't the way it should happen," he said with some difficulty.

"What is the way?"

"Like this: if ever there was an earthquake, or I looked up and saw a safe falling on me, or some other thing like that, something from outside myself—I wouldn't move aside. I'd let it happen."

"Is there a difference between that and shooting yourself?"

"Yes!" he said, with more animation than he had shown so far. "Put it like this: there's part of me that's dead, and wants the rest of me dead. There's a part of me that's alive, and wants all of me alive." He looked that over and nodded at it. "My hand, my arm, my thumb on the trigger—they're alive. All the live parts of me want to help me go on living, d'you see? No live part should help the dead part get what it wants. The way it'll happen, the way it should happen, is not when I do something to make it happen. It'll be when I don't do something. I won't get out of the way, and that's it, and thanks for keeping the gun for me, it's no use to me." He stood up and found his eyes locked with hers, and sat right down again, breathing hard.

"Why do you want to be dead?" she asked flatly.

He put his head down on his hands and began to rock it slowly to and fro.

"Don't you want to know?"

Muffled, his voice came up from the edge of the table. "No." Abruptly he sat up, staring. "No? What made me say no? Bitty," he demanded, "what made me say that?"

She shrugged. He jumped up and began pacing swiftly up and down the kitchen. "I'll be dogged," he murmured once, and "Well, what d'ye kn—"

Bitty watched him, and catching him on a turn when their eyes could meet, she asked, "Well,—why do you want to—"

"Shut up," he said. He said it, not to her, but to any interruption. His figmentary signal-light, which indicated dissatisfaction, unrightness, was casting its glow all over his interior landscape. To be hounded half to death by something like this, then to discover that basically he didn't want to investigate it. . . . He sat down and faced her, his eyes alight. "I don't know yet," he said, "but I will, I will." He took a deep breath. "It's like being chased by something that's gaining on you, and you duck into an alley, and then you find it's blind, there's only a brick wall; so you sit down to wait, it's all you can do. And all of a sudden you find a door in the wall. Been there all the time. Just didn't look."

"Why do you want to be dead?"

"B-because I—I shouldn't be alive. Because the average guy—Different, that's what I am, different, unfit."

"Different, unfit." Bitty's eyebrows raised slightly. "They the same thing, Philip?"

"Well, sure."

"You can't jump like a kangaroo, you can't

eat grass raw like a cow—different. You unfit because you can't do those things?"

He made an annoyed laugh. "Not that, not that. People, I mean."

"You can't fly a plane. You can't sing like Sue Martin. You can't spout law like Tony O'Banion. That kind of different?"

"No," he said, and in a surge of anguish, "No, no! I can't talk about it, Bitty!" He looked at her and again saw that rare, deep smile. He answered it in kind, but weakly, remembering that he had said that to her before. "This time I mean I can't talk about such things to you. To a lady," he said in abrupt, unbearable confusion.

"I'm no lady," said Bitty with conviction. Suddenly she punched his forearm; he thought it was the first time she had ever touched him. "To you I'm not even a human being. Not even another person. I mean it," she said warmly. "Have I asked you a single question you couldn't've asked yourself? Have I told you anything you didn't know?"

His peculiar linear mind cast rapidly back and up again. He felt an odd instant of disorientation. It was not unpleasant. Bitty said gently, "Go on talking to yourself, boy. Who knows—you might find yourself in good company."

"Aw . . . thanks, Bitty," he mumbled. His eyes stung and he shook his head. "All right, all *right*, then . . . it just came to me, one big flash, and I guess I couldn't sit here—here," he said, waving his arm to include the scrubbed, friendly kitchen, "and look at you, and think about

these—uh this—all at once." He swallowed heavily. "Well, that time I told you about, that day I found out I wanted to be dead, it was like getting hit on the head. Right after that, only a couple of minutes, I got hit on the head just as hard by something else. I didn't know—want to know till now that they were connected, some way." He closed his eyes. "It was a theater, that rathole down across the Circle. You know. It—it hit out at me when I wasn't looking. It was all covered with . . . pictures and—and it said SEE this and SEE that and SEE some dirty other thing, adults only, you know what I mean." He opened his eyes to see what Bitty was doing, but Bitty was doing nothing at all. Waiting. He turned his face away from her, and said indistinctly into his shoulder, "All my life those things meant nothing to me. *There!*" he shouted, "you see? Different, different!"

But she wouldn't see. Or she wouldn't see until he did, himself, more clearly. She still waited.

He said, "Down at work, there's a fellow, Scodie. This Scodie, he's a good man, really can turn out a day's work. I mean, he likes what he's doing, he cares. Except every time a girl goes by, everything stops. He snaps up out of what he's doing, he watches her. I mean, *every* time. It's like he can't help himself. He does it the way a cadet salutes an officer on the street. He does it like that crossing-guard on the toy train, that pops out of his little house every time his little light goes on. He watches until the girl's gone by, and then he says 'mmm*yuh!*' and looks over at me and winks."

"What do you do, every time?"

"Well, I—" He laughed uncertainly. "I guess I wink back at him and I say, mm-*hm*! But I know why I do it, it's because he expects me to; he'd think it was sort of peculiar if I didn't. But he doesn't do it for me; I don't expect anything of him one way or the other. He does it—" Words failed him, and he tried again. "Doing that, he's part of—everybody. What he does is the same thing every song on every radio says every minute. Every ad in every magazine does it if it possibly can, even if it means a girl in her underwear with stillson wrenches for sale." He leapt to his feet and began to pace excitedly. "You got to back off a little to see it," he told Bitty, who smiled behind his back. "You got to look at the whole thing all at once, to see how *much* there is of it, the jokes people tell—yeah, you got to laugh at them, whatever, you even have to know a couple, or they'll . . . The window displays, the television, the movies . . . somebody's writing an article about transistors or termites or something, and every once in a while he figures he's been away from it long enough and he has to say something about the birds and the bees and 'Gentlemen prefer.' Everywhere you turn the whole world's at it, chipping and chipping away at it—"

He stamped back to the table and looked into Bitty's face intently. "You got to back away and look at it all at once," he cautioned again. "I'm not in kindergarten, I know what it's all about. I'm not a woman-hater. I've been in love. I'll get married, some day. Go ahead and tell me I'm talking about one of the biggest, strongest,

down-deep urges we have—I'll buy that. That's what I *mean*, that's what I'm *talking* about." His forehead was pink and shiny; he took out a crumpled handkerchief and battled at it. "So *much* of it, all around you, all the time, filling a big hungry need in average people. I don't mean the urge itself; I mean all this *reminding*, this what do you call it, indoctrination. It's a need or folks wouldn't stand for so much of it, comic books, lipstick, that air-jet in the floor at the funny house at the Fair." He thumped into his chair, panting. "Do you begin to see what I mean about '*different*'?"

"Do you?" asked Bitty, but Halvorsen didn't hear her; he was talking again. "Different, because I don't feel that hunger to be reminded, I don't need all that high-pressure salesmanship, I don't want it. Every time I tell one of my jokes, every time I wink back at old Scodie, I feel like a fool, like some sort of liar. But you got to protect yourself; you can't ever let anyone find out. You know why? Because the average guy, the guy-by-the-millions that needs all that noise so much, he'll let you be the way he is, or he'll let you be ... I'm sorry, Bitty. Don't make me go into a lot of dirty details. You see what I mean, don't you?"

"What do you mean?"

Irritated, he blew a single sharp blast from his nostrils. "Well, what I mean is, they'll let you be the way they are, or you have to be ... sick, crippled. You can't be anything else! You can't be Phil Halvorsen who isn't sick and who isn't crippled but who just doesn't naturally go

around banging his antlers against the rocks so the whole world can hear it."

"So—that's what you mean by unfit?"

"That's why I wanted to be dead. I just don't think the way other people do; if I act the way other people do I feel . . . feel guilty. I guess I had this piling up in me for years, and that day with the guns, when I found out what I wanted to do . . . and then that theater-front, yawping over me like a wet mouth full of dirty teeth . . ." He giggled foolishly. "Listen to me, will you . . . Bitty, I'm sorry."

She utterly ignored this. "High-pressure salesmanship," she said.

"What?"

"You said it, I didn't . . . Isn't hunger one of those big deep needs, Philip? Suppose you had a bunch of folks starving on an island and dropped them a ton of food—would they need high-pressure salesmanship?"

It was as if he stood at the edge of a bottomless hole—more, the very outer edge of the world, so close his very toes projected over the emptiness. It filled him with wonder; he was startled, but not really afraid, because it might well be that to fall down and down into that endless place might be a very peaceful thing. He closed his eyes and slowly, very slowly, came back to reality, the kitchen. Bitty, Bitty's words. "You mean . . . the av—the ordin—you mean, people aren't really interested?"

"Not that interested."

He blinked; he felt as if he had ceased to exist in his world and had been plunked down in a

very similar, but totally new one. It was far less lonely here.

He hit the table and laughed into Bitty's calm face. "I'm going to sleep," he said, and got up; and he knew she had caught his exact shade of meaning when she said gently, "Sure you can."

EXCERPT FROM FIELD EXPEDITION [NOTEBOOK]: [I] had thought up to now that in [Smith]'s [immorally] excessive enthusiasm and [bullheadedness] [I] had encountered the utmost in [irritants]. [I] was in [error]; [he] now surpasses these, and without effort. In the first place, having placated and outwitted the alerted specimen, [he] has destroyed [my] preliminary detailed [report] on him; this is [irritat]ing not only because it was done without consulting [me], not only because of the trouble [I] went to [write] it all up, but mostly because [he] is technically within [his] [ethics-rights]—the emergency created by [his] [bumbling mismanagement] no longer exists. [I] have [force]fully pointed out to [him] that it was only by the application of [my] kind of cautious resourcefulness that [he] succeeded, but [he] just [gloats]. [I] [most strongly affirm-and-bind-myself], the instant [we] get back home and are released from Expeditionary [ethic-discipline], [I] shall [bend] [his] [   ]s over [his] [   ] and [tie a knot in] them.

[We] have now, no [credit-thanks] to [Smith], reached a point where all our specimens are in a state of [heavy] preconditioning of their unaccountably random Synapse Beta sub Sixteen. Being a synapse, it will of course come

into full operation only on a reflexive level and in an extreme emergency, which [we] are now setting up.

Unless [Smith] produces yet more [stupidities], the specimens should live through this.

X

It had become impossibly hot, and very still. Leaves dropped at impossible angles, and still the dust lay on them. Sounds seemed too enervated to travel very far. The sky was brass all day, and at night, for want of ambition, the overcast was no more than a gauzy hood of haze.

It was the Bittelmans' "day off" again, and without them the spine had been snatched out of the household. The boarders ate pokily, lightly, at random, and somehow got through the time when there was nothing to do but sit up late enough to get tired enough to get whatever rest the temperature would permit. It was too hot, even, to talk, and no one attempted it. They drifted to their rooms to wait for sleep; they slumped in front of the fans and took cold showers which generated more heat than they dissipated. When at last darkness came, it was a relief only to the eyes. The household pulse beat slowly and slower; by eight o'clock it was library-quiet, by nine quite silent, so that the soft brushing of knuckles on Miss Schmidt's door struck her like a shout.

"Wh-who is it?" she quavered, when she recovered her breath.

"Sue."

"Oh—oh. Oh, do come in." She pulled the damp sheet tight up against her throat.

"Oh, you're in bed already. I'm sorry."

"*I'm* sorry. It's all right."

Sue Martin swung the door shut and came all the way in. She was wearing an off-the-shoulder peasant blouse and a pleated skirt with three times more filmy nylon in it than one would guess until she turned, when it drifted like smoke. "My," said Miss Schmidt enviously. "You look cool."

"State of mind," Sue smiled. "I'm about to go to work and I wish I didn't have to."

"And Bitty's out. I'm honorary baby-sitter again."

"You're an angel."

"No, oh, no!" cried Miss Schmidt.

"I wish everything I had to do was that easy. Why, in all the time I've known you, every time I've done it, I—I've had nothing to do!"

"He sleeps pretty soundly. Clear conscience, I guess."

"I think it's because he's happy. He smiles when he sleeps."

"Smiles? Sometimes he laughs out loud," said Sue Martin. "I was a little worried tonight, for a while. He was so flushed and wide-awake—"

"Well, it's *hot*."

"It wasn't that." Sue chuckled. "His precious Boff was all over the place, 'fixin' things,' Robin said. What he was fixing all over the walls and ceiling, Robin didn't say. Whatever it was, it's finished now, though, and Robin's sound asleep. I'm sure you won't even have to go in. And Bitty ought to be home soon."

"You'll leave your door open?"

Sue Martin nodded and glanced up at the large open transom over Miss Schmidt's door. "You'll hear him if he so much as blinks. . . . I've got to run. Thanks *so* much."

"Oh, really, Mrs. M—uh, Sue. Don't thank me. Just run along."

"Good night."

Sue Martin slipped out, silently closing the door behind her. Miss Schmidt sighed and looked up at the transom. After Sue's light footsteps had faded away, she listened, listened as hard as she could, trying to pour part of herself through the transom, across the hall, through Sue Martin's open door. A light sleeper at any time, she knew confidently that she was on guard now and would wake if anything happened. If she slept at all in this sticky heat.

She might sleep, at that, she thought after a while. She shifted herself luxuriously, and edged to a slightly cooler spot on the bed. "That wicked Sam," she murmured, and blushed in the dark. But he had been right. A *nightgown* in weather like this?

Suddenly, she slept.

In O'Banion's room, there was a soft sound. He had put off taking a shower until suddenly he had used up his energy, and could hardly stir. I'll just rest my eyes, he thought, and bowed his head. The soft sound was made by his forehead striking the book.

Halvorsen lay rigid on his bed, staring at the ceiling. There, almost as if it was projected, was the image of a flimsy cylinder vomiting smoke. Go ahead, he thought, detachedly. Or go away.

I don't care which. Before I talked to Bitty, I wanted you. Now, I don't care. Is that better? He closed his eyes, but the image was still there. He lay very quietly, watching the insides of his eyelids. It was like being asleep. When he was asleep the thing was there too.

Mary Haunt sat by her window, pretending it was cooler there than in bed. There was no anger in her, just now as she lay back and dreamed. The Big Break, the pillars of light at her première, her name two stories tall over a Broadway marquee—these had no place in this particular favorite dream. I'll do over Mom's room, she thought, dimity, this time, and full, full skirts on the vanity and the night table. She closed her eyes, putting herself in Mom's room with such vividness that she could almost smell the cool faint odor of lavender sachets and the special freshness of sheets dried in the sun. Yes, and something else, outside the room, barely, just barely she knew bread was baking, so that the kitchen would be heavenly with it; the bread would dominate the spice-shelf for a while, until it was out of the oven and cooled. "Oh, Mom ..." she whispered. She lay still in her easy-chair, holding and holding to the vision until this room, this house, this town didn't matter any more.

Some hours went by.

Robin floated in a luminous ocean of sleep where there was nothing to fear and where, if he just turned to look, there were love and laughter waiting for him. His left hand uncurled and he thrust the second and third fingers together into his mouth. Somehow he was

a big bulldozer with a motor that sounded like Mitster and tracks that clattered along like Coffeepot, and Boff and Googie were riding along with him and laughing. Then without effort he was a glittery ferris-wheel, but he could watch himself too in one of the cars, screaming his delight and leaning against Tonio's hard arm. All this, yet he was still afloat in that deep bright place where there was no fear, where love and laughter hid around some indescribable corner, waiting. Bright, brighter. Warm, warm, warmer . . . oh, hot *hot!*

XI

Miss Schmidt opened her eyes to an impossible orange glare and a roar like the end of the world. For one full second she lay still, paralyzed by an utter disbelief; no light could have become so bright, no sound could have risen to this volume, without waking her as it began. Then she found a way to focus her eyes against the radiance, and saw the flames, and in what was left to her of her immobile second, she explained the whole thing to herself and said redly, of course, of course; it's only a nightmare and *suppose there's a fire?*—and that's so *silly,* Sam—

And then she was out of bed in a single bound, standing in the center of the room, face to flaming face with reality. Everything was burning—everything! The drapes had already gone and the slats of the venetian blind, their cords gone, were heaped on the floor, going like a campfire. Even as she watched the screen sagged and

crumpled, its pine frame glaring and spitting pitch through blistering paint. It fell outside.

Outside, outside! The window's open, you're on the ground floor; yes, and there on the chair, not burning yet, your bathrobe; take the robe and jump, quick!

Then, beyond belief, there was a sound louder than the earth-filling roar, and different; fine hot powder and a hot hail of plaster showered on her shoulders; she looked up to see the main beam, right over her head, sag toward her and hang groaning, one part reaching to the other with broken flat fingers of splintered wood which gloved themselves in flame as she saw them. She cowered, and just then the handle of the door turned and a gout of smoke slammed it open and whisked out of sight in the updraft; and there in the hall stood Robin, grinding a fat little fist into one abruptly wakened eye. She could see his lips move, though she could hear nothing in this mighty bellow of sound. She knew it, though, and heard it clearly in her mind: "What's 'at noice?"

The beam overhead grumbled and again she was showered with plaster. She batted it off her shoulders, and whimpered. A great flame must have burst from the roof above her just then, for through the window she saw a brilliant glare reflected from the white clapboards of the garage wall outside. The glare tugged at her—*jump!*—and besides, her robe . . .

The beam thundered and began to fall. Now she must make a choice, in microseconds. The swiftest thought would not be fast enough to weigh and consider and decide; all that could

matter now was what was inside her, throwing
switches (some so worn and easy to move!). A
giant was throwing them, and he was strong;
his strength was a conditioning deeper than
thou shalt not kill; he was a lesson learned before she had learned to love God, or to walk, or
to talk. He was her mother's authority and the
fear of all the hairy, sweaty, dangerous mys-
teries from which she had shielded herself all
her life; and his name and title were Cover Thyself! With him, helping him, was the reflexive
Save Thyself! and against these—Robin, whom
she loved (but love is what she felt, once, for a
canary, and once for a Raggedy Ann doll) and
her sense of duty to Sue Martin (but so lightly
promised, and at the time such a meaningless
formality). There could be no choice in such a
battle, though she must live with the conse-
quences for all her years.

Then—

—it was as if a mighty voice had called *Stop!*
and the very flames froze. Half a foot above her
hung the jagged end of the burning beam, and
chunks of plaster, splinters and scraps of shat-
tered lath and glowing joist stopped in midair.
Yet during this sliver of a fraction of time, she
knew that the phenomenon was a mental something, a figment, and the idea of time-cessation
only a clumsy effort of her mind's to account
for what was happening.

Save Thyself was still there, hysterical hands
clutching for the controls, but *Cover Thyself*
disappeared into the background. Save herself
she would, but it would be on new terms. She
was in the grip of a reflex of reflexes, one which

took into consideration all the factors a normal reflex would, to the end goal of survival. But along with these, it called up everything Reta Schmidt had ever done, everything she had been. In a single soundless flash, a new kind of light was thrown into every crevice and cranny of her existence. It was her total self now, reacting to a total situation far wider than that which obtained here in this burning room. It illuminated even the future—that much of it which depended upon these events, between them and the next probable major "crossroads." It canceled past misjudgments and illogics and replaced them with rightness, even for the times she had known what was right and had done otherwise. It came and was gone even while she leaped, while she took two bounding steps across the floor and the beam crashed and crushed and showered sparks where she had been standing.

She scooped up the child and ran down the hall, through the foyer, into the kitchen. It was dark there, thick with swirling smoke, but the glass panels on the kitchen door glared with some unfamiliar light from outdoors. She began to cough violently, but grimly aimed at the light and drove ahead. It was eclipsed suddenly by a monstrous shadow, and suddenly it exploded inward. There were lights out there she had never seen before, and half-silhouetted in the broken doorway was a big man with a gleaming helmet and an axe. She tried to call, or perhaps it was only a scream, but instead she went into a spasm of coughing.

"Somebody in here?" asked the man. A beam

of light, apparently from the street, lit up the shield on the front of his helmet as he leaned forward. He stepped inside. "Whew! Where are you?"

She went blindly to him and pushed Robin against his coat. "The baby," she croaked. "Get him out of this smoke."

He grunted and suddenly Robin was gone from her arms. "You all right?" He was peering into the black and the smoke.

"Take him out," she said. "Then I'll want your coat."

He went out. Miss Schmidt could hear Robin's clear voice: "You a fireman?"

"I sure am," rumbled the man. "Want to see my fire engine? Then sit right there on the grass and wait one second. Okay?"

"Okay."

The coat flew through the doorway.

"Got it?"

"Thank you." She put the huge garment on and went out. The fireman waited there, again holding Robin in his arms. "You all right, ma'am?"

Her lungs were an agony and she had burns on her feet and shoulders. Her hair was singed and one of her hands was flayed across its back. "I'm just fine," she said.

They began to walk up the road. Robin squirmed around in the man's arms and popped his head out to look back at the brightly burning house.

" 'By, Boff," he said happily, and then gave his heart to the fire engine.

XII

"Mother, the bread's burning!"

Mary Haunt opened her eyes to an impossible glare and a great roaring. She shrieked and flailed out blindly, as if she could frighten it away, whatever it was; and then she came enough to her senses to realize that she still sat in her chair by the window, and that the house was on fire. She leaped to her feet, sending the heavy chair skittering across the room where it toppled over against the clothespress. As it always did when it was bumped, the clothespress calmly opened its doors.

But Mary Haunt didn't wait for that or anything else. She struck the screen with the flat of her hand. It popped out easily, and she hit the ground almost at the same time as it did. She ran off a few steps, and then, like Lot's wife, curiosity overtook her and she stopped. She turned around in fascination.

Great wavering flames leapt fifty and sixty feet in the air and all the windows were alight. From the town side she could hear the shriek and clang of fire engines, and the windows and doors opening, and running feet. But the biggest sound of all was the roar of the fire, like a giant's blowtorch.

She looked back at her own window. She could see into the room easily, the chair on its side, the bed with its chenille top-spread sprouting measles of spark and char, and the gaping doors of the—"My clothes! My clothes!"

Furiously she ran back to the window, paused a moment in horror to see fire run along the

picture-molding of the inside wall like a nightmare caterpillar. "My clothes," she whispered. She didn't make much money at her job, but every cent that wasn't used in bed and board went on her back. She mouthed something, and from her throat came that animal growl of hers; she put both hands on the sill and leaped, and tumbled back into the house.

She was prepared for the heat but not for that intensity of light, and the noise was worst of all. She recoiled from it and stood for a moment with her hands over her eyes, swaying with the impact of it. Then she ground her teeth and made her way across to the clothespress. She swept open the bottom drawer and turned out the neatly folded clothes. Down at the bottom was a cotton print dress, wrapped carefully around a picture frame. She lifted it out and hugged it, and ran across to the window with it. She leaned far out and dropped it gently on the grass, then turned back in again.

The far wall, by the door, began to buckle high up, and suddenly there was fire up there. The corner near the ceiling toppled into the room with a crash and a cloud of white dust and greasy-looking smoke, and then the whole wall fell, not toward her, but away, so that her room now included a section of the corridor outside. As the dust settled somebody, a man, came roaring inarticulately and battering through the rubble. She could not know who it was. He apparently meant to travel the corridor whether it was all there or not, and he did, disappearing again into the inferno.

She staggered back toward the clothespress.

She felt mad, drunk, crazy. Maybe it was the de-oxygenated atmosphere and maybe it was fear and reaction, but it was sort of wonderful, too; she felt her face writhing and part of her was numb with astonishment at what the rest of her was doing; she was laughing. She slammed into the clothespress, gasping for breath, filled her lungs and delivered up a shrill peal of laughter. Almost helpless from it, she fumbled down a dull satin evening gown with a long silver sash. She held it up in front of her and laughed again, doubling over it, and then straightened up, rolling the dress up into a ball as she did so. With all her might she hurled it into the rubble of the hallway. Next was a simple black dress with no back and a little bolero; with an expression on her face that can only be described as cheerful, she threw it after the evening gown. Then the blue, and the organdy with the taffeta underskirt, and the black and orange one she used to call her Hallowe'en dress; each one she dragged out, held up, and hurled: "You," she growled between her convulsions of laughter, "you, and you, and *you*." When the press was empty, she ran to the bureau and snatched open her scarf drawer, uncovering a flowerbed of dainty, filmy silk and nylon and satin shawls, scarves, and kerchiefs. She whipped out an over-sized babushka, barely heavier than the air that floated it, and ran with it to the flaming mass where her door once was. She dipped and turned like a dancer, fluttering it through flame, and when it was burning sh bounced back to the bureau and put it in t'

drawer with the others. Fire streamed out of the drawer and she laughed and laughed . . .

And something nipped her sharply on the calves; she yelped and turned and found the lace of her black negligee was on fire. She twisted back and gathered the cloth and ripped it away. The pain had sobered her and she was bewildered now, weak and beginning to be frightened. She started for the window and tripped and fell heavily, and when she got up the smoke was suddenly like a scalding blanket over her head and shoulders and she didn't know which way to go. She knelt and peered and found the window in an unexpected direction, and made for it. As she tumbled through, the ceiling behind her fell, and the roof after it.

On her belly she clawed away from the house, sobbing, and at last rose to her knees. She smelt of smoke and burned hair and all her lovely fingernails were broken. She squatted on the ground, staring at the flaming shell of the house, and cried like a little girl. But when her swollen eyes rested on that square patch in the grass, she stopped crying and got up and limped over to it. Her cotton print, and the picture . . . she picked the tidy package up and went tiredly away with it into the shadows where the hedge met the garage.

XIII

O'Banion raised his head groggily from the flyleaf of his *Blackstone* and the neat inscription written there:

The law doth punish man or woman
That steals the goose from off the common,
But let the greater felon loose,
That steals the common from the goose,

—a piece of Eighteenth Century japery which O'Banion deplored. However, it had been written there by Opdycke when he was in law school, and the Opdyckes were a darn fine family. Princeton people, of course, but nobody minded.

All this flickered through his mind as he swam up out of sleep, along with "What's the matter with my head?" because any roaring that loud must be in his ears; it would be too incredible anywhere else, and "What's the matter with the light?"

Then he was fully awake, and on his feet. "My God!"

He ran to the door and snatched it open. Flame squirted at him as if from a hose; in a split second he felt his eyebrows disappear. He yelled and staggered back from it, and it pursued him. He turned and dove out the window, landing clumsily on his stomach with his fists clenched over his solar plexus. His own weight drove the fists deep, and for a full minute he lay groaning for air. At last he got up, shook himself, and pelted around the house to the front. One fire engine was already standing by the curb. There was a police car and the knot of bug-eyed spectators who spring apparently out of the ground at the scene of any accident anywhere at any hour. At the far end of the Bittelman lot, there was a sharp scream of rubber

and a glare of lights as a taxicab pulled in as close to the police barrier as it could get. The door was already open; a figure left it, half running, half thrown out by the sudden stop.

"*Sue!*" But no one heard him—everyone else was yelling too: "Look!" "Somebody stop her!" "Hey!" "Hey, you!"

O'Banion backed off a little to cup his hands and yell again, when directly over his head a cheerful small voice said, "Mommy runs *fast!*"

"Robin! You're all right—" He was perched on top of the fire engine with one arm around the shining brass bell, looking like a Botticelli seraph. Someone beside him—good heavens, it was Miss Schmidt, disheveled and bright-eyed, wrapped up in some tentlike garment—Miss Schmidt screamed, "Stop her, stop her, I've got the baby here!"

Robin said to Miss Schmidt, "Tonio runs fast too, shall we?"

Now they were all yelling at O'Banion, but in four paces he could hear nothing but the roar ahead of him. He had never seen a house burn like this, all over, all at once. He took the porch steps in one bound and had just time to turn his shoulder to the door. It was ajar, but couldn't swing fast enough under such an impact. It went down flat and slid, and for one crazy moment O'Banion was riding it like an aquaplane in a sea of fire, for the foyer floor was ablaze. Then the leading edge of the door caught on something and spilled him off. He rolled over twice in fuming debris and then got his feet under him. It was like a particularly bad dream, so familiar, so confusing. He turned

completely around to orient himself, found the
corridor, and started up it, yelling for Sue at
the top of his voice. He saw a left-hand wall
lean down toward him and had to scamper back
out of the way. It had barely poured its rubble
down when he was on, in, and through it. Over
the crash and roar, over his own hoarse bel-
ing, he thought he heard a crazy woman
laughing somewhere in the fire. Even in his
near-hysteria, he could say, "Not Sue, that's not
Sue Martin. . . ." And he was, before he knew it,
at and past Sue Martin's room. He flung out a
hand. He bounced off the end wall and turned
as he did so, like a sprint swimmer, and swung
into Sue Martin's room. "Sue! Sue!"

Was he mistaken? Did someone call, "Robin—
Robin honey . . ."?

He dropped to his knees, where he could see
in relatively clearer air. "Sue, oh Sue!"

She lay half buried in rubble from the fallen
ceiling. He threw off scorched and broken two-
by-fours and burning lath, took her by the
shoulders and lifted her out of the heap of broken plaster—thank the powers for that! it had
protected her to some degree. "Sue?"

"Robin," she croaked.

He shook her. "He's all right, he's outside, I
saw him."

She opened her eyes and frowned at him. Not
at him; at what he had said. "He's here somewhere."

"I saw him. Come on!" He lifted her to her
feet, and as she dragged, "It's the truth; do you
think *I* would lie to you?"

He felt strength surge into her body. "You

forgot to say, 'I, an O'Banion,' " she said, but it didn't hurt. They stumbled to the window and he pushed her through it and leaped after her. For two painful breaths they lay gulping clean air, and then O'Banion got to his feet. His head was spinning and he almost lay down again. He set his jaw and helped Sue Martin up. "Too close!" he shouted. Holding her up, he half-dragged her no more than a step when she suddenly straightened, and with unexpected and irresistible strength leapt back toward the burning wall, pulling him with her. He caught at her to regain his balance, and she put her arms tight around him. "The wall!" he screamed, as it leaned out over them. She said nothing, but her arms tightened even more, and he could have moved more easily if he had been bound to a post with steel chains. The wall came down then, thunder and sparks, like the end of the world; madly, it occurred to him just then that he could solve one of his problem cases by defining the unorthodox contract under suit as a stock certificate.

But instead of dying he took a stinging blow on his right shoulder, and that was all. He opened his eyes. He and Sue Martin still stood locked together, and all around them was flame like a flower-bed with the rough outline of the house wall and its peaked roof. Around their feet was the four-foot circular frame of the attic vent, which had ringed them like a quoit.

The woman slumped in his arms, and he lifted her and picked his way, staggering, into the friendly dark and the welcome hands of the firemen. But when they tried to lift her away from

him she held his arm and would not let go. "Put me down, just put me down," she said. "I'm all right. Put me down."

They did and she leaned against O'Banion. He said, "We're okay now. We'll go up to the road. Don't mind about us." The firemen hesitated, but when they began to walk, they were apparently reassured, and ran back to their work. Hopeless work, O'Banion amended. But for a few sagging studs and the two chimneys, the house was little more than a pit of flames.

"Is Robin really—"

"Shh. He's really. Miss Schmidt got him out, I think. Anyway, he's sitting on the fire engine enjoying every minute. He watched you going in. He approves of your speed."

"You—"

"I saw you too. I yelled."

"And then you came after me." They walked a slow pace or so. "Why?"

Robin was safe, of course, he was about to say, so you didn't have to—and then there was within him a soundless white flash that lit up all he had ever done and been, everything he had read, people and places and ideas. Where he had acted right, he felt the right proven; where he had been wrong, he could see now the right in full force, even when for years he had justified his wrong. He saw fully now what old Sam Bittelman had almost convinced him of intellectually with his searching questions. He had fought away Sam's suggestion that there was something ludicrous, contradictory about the law and its pretensions to permanence. Now he saw that the law, as he knew it, was not un-

der attack at all. As long as a man treated the body of law like a great stone buttress, based in bedrock and propping up civilization, he was fortifying a dead thing which could only kill the thing it was built to uphold. But if he saw civilization as an intricate, *moving entity*, the function of law changed. It was governor, stabilizer, inhibitor, *control* of something dynamic and progressive, subject to the punishments and privileges of evolution like a living thing. His whole idea of the hair-splitting search for "precedent" as a refining process in law was wrong. It was an adaptive process instead. The suggestion that not one single law is common to all human cultures, past and present, was suddenly no insult to law at all, but a living compliment; to nail a culture to permanent laws now seemed as ridiculous a concept as man conventionally refusing to shed his scales and his gills.

And with this revelation of the viability of man and his works, O'Banion experienced a profound realignment in his (or was it really his) attitude toward himself, his effortful pre-occupation to defend and justify his blood and breeding and his gentleman's place in the world. It came to him now that although the law may say here that men are born equal, and there that they must receive equal treatment before the law, no one but a complete fool would insist that men *are* equal. Men, wherever they come from, whatever they claim for themselves, are only what's in their heads and what's in their hearts. The purest royal blood that yields a weak king will yield a failure; a strong peasant

can rise higher and accomplish more, and if what he accomplishes is compatible with human good, he is surely no worse than a beneficent king. Over and above anything else, however, shone the fact that a good man needs least of all to prove it by claiming that he comes from a line of good men. And for him to assume the privileges and postures of the landed gentry after the land is gone is pure buffoonery. Time enough for sharp vertical differentiations between men when the differences become so great that the highest may not cross-breed with the lowest; until then, in the broad view, differences are so subtle as to be negligible, and the concept "to marry out of one's class" belongs with the genesis of hippogriffs and gryphons— in mythology.

All this, and a thousand times more, unfolded and was clear to O'Banion in this illuminated instant, so short it took virtually no time at all, so bright it lit up all the days of his past and part of his future as well. And it had happened between pace and pace, when Sue Martin said, "You followed me. Why?"

"I love you," he said instantly.

"Why?" she whispered.

He laughed joyously. "It doesn't matter."

Sue Martin—*Sue Martin!*—began to cry.

XIV

Phil Halvorsen opened his eyes and saw that the house was on fire. He lay still, watching the flames feed, and thought, isn't this what I was waiting for?

Now there can be an end to it, he thought peacefully. Now I never need worry again that I'm wrong to be as I am, and other people's needs, the appetites and rituals of the great Average will no longer accuse me. I cannot be excluded unless I exist, so here's an end to being excluded. I cannot be looked down on when I can no longer be seen.

The ceiling began to develop a tan patch, and hot white powder fell from it to his face. He covered it with the pillow. He was resigned to later, final agonies because they would be final, but he saw no reason to put up with the preliminaries. Just then most of the plaster came down on him. It didn't hurt much, and it meant the thing would be over sooner than he thought.

He heard faintly, over the colossal roaring, a woman scream. He lay still. As much as anyone—perhaps more—he would ordinarily be concerned about the others. But not now. Not now. Such concern is for a man who expects to live with a conscience afterward.

Something—it sounded like an inside wall—went down very near. It jolted the foot of his bed and he felt its hot exhalation and the taste of its soot, but otherwise it did not reach him. "So come on," he said tightly, "get it over with, will you?" and hurled the pillow away.

As if in direct and obedient answer the ceiling over him opened up—*up;* apparently a beam had broken and was tipping down into an adjoining room, upward here. Then the tangle of stringers it carried fell away and started down. High above was blackness, suddenly rent by

smoky orange light—inside of the roof, a section of which was falling in with the stringers.

"All right," said Halvorsen, as if someone had asked him a question. He closed his eyes.

He closed his eyes on a flash of something like an inner and unearthly light, and time stood still . . . or perhaps it was only that subjectively he had all the time in the world to examine this shadowless internal cosmos.

Most immediately, it laid out before him the sequence of events which had brought him here, awaiting death on a burning bed. In this sequence a single term smote him with that "well, of *course!*" revelation that rewarded his plodding, directive thoughts when they were successful for him. The term was "Average," and his revelation came like a burst of laughter: for anyone else this would have been a truism, an inarguable axiom; like a fool he had let his convoluted thinking breeze past "Average," use "Average," worry about "Average" without ever looking at it.

But "Average"—Average Appetite—was here for him to see, a line drawn from side to side on a huge graph. And all over the graph were spots—millions of them. (He was in a place where he could actually see and comprehend "millions".) On that line lived this creation, this demigod, to whom he had felt subservient for so long, whose hungers and whose sense of fitness ought to have been—*had* been—Halvorsen's bench-mark, his reference point. Halvorsen had always felt himself member of a minority—a minority which shrank as he examined it, and he was always examining it. All the world

catered to Average Man and his "normal" urges, and this must be proper, for he was aware of the reciprocities: Average Man got these things because these things were what Average Man wanted and needed.

Want and need . . . and there was the extraordinary discovery he had made when Bitty asked him: if people really needed it, would there have to be so much high-pressure salesmanship?

This he threw on the graph like a transparent overlay; it too bore a line from side to side, but much lower down, indicating with much more accuracy just how interested Average Man was in the specific appetite about which he made so much noise. Now bend close and look at those millions of spots—individual people all, each with his true need for the kind of cultural pressure which was driving a man, here, to his death from guilt.

The first thing Halvorsen saw was that the dots were scattered so widely that the actual number falling on the line Average Man was negligible: there were countless millions more un-average people. It came to him that those who obey the gospel of Average Man are, in their efforts to be like the mass of humanity, obeying the dictates of one of the smallest minorities of all. The next thing to strike him was that it took the presence of *all* these dots to place that line just where it was; there was no question of better, or worse, or more or less fit. Except for the few down here and their opposite numbers up there, the handful of sick, insane, incomplete or distorted individuals whose sexual appetites were non-existent or extreme,

the vast majority above and below the true average were basically "normal." And here where he, Halvorsen might appear on the graph—he had plenty of company.

He'd never known that! The magazine covers, the advertisements, the dirty jokes—they hadn't let him know it.

He understood now, the mechanism of this cultural preoccupation; it came to him in the recollection that he had appeared at work for three hundred consecutive working days and nobody noticed his ears. And then one day a sebaceous cyst in his left lobe had become infected, and the doctor removed it and he showed up at work with a bandage covering his ear. *Everybody began to think about Halvorsen's ear!* Every interview had to begin with an explanation of his ear or the applicant would keep straying his attention to it. And he'd noticed, too, that after he explained about the cyst, the interviewee would always glance at Halvorsen's other ear before he got back to business. Now, in this silver place where all interrelationships were true ones, he could equate his covered and noticeable ear with a Bikini bathing suit, and see clearly how normal interest-disinterest—acceptance—can be put under forced draft.

It came to him also *why* this particular cultural matrix did this to itself. In its large subconscious, it probably knew quite clearly the true status of its sensual appetites. It must reason, then, that unless it kept these appetites whipped up to a froth at all times, it might not increase itself, and it felt it must increase. This

was not a pretty thought, but neither is the pounce of a cat on a baby bird; yet one cannot argue with the drive behind it.

So it was that Halvorsen's reasons for not living ceased to be reasons; with the purest of truth he could say I am not unmanned; I am not unfit; I am not abnormal . . . I am not alone.

All this in no-time, as he closed his eyes to await the mass even now falling on him. And the reflex of reflexes acted just as eyelids met; he spun off the bed, bounced out of the nearby window, and was on the grass outside as the ceiling and walls together met the floor in a gout of flame.

XV

The girl climbed up to the front seat of the fire engine. "Move over."

Miss Schmidt swung her worried gaze away from the burning house, and said in a preoccupied tone, "I don't think you'd be allowed to, little girl. We're from that hou—why, it's Mary Haunt!"

"Didn't recognize me, huh?" said Mary Haunt. She swung a hip and shunted Miss Schmidt over. "Can't say I blame you. What a mess!" she said, indicating the house.

"Mr. O'Banion is in there; he went after Mrs. Martin. And have you seen Mr. Halvorsen?"

"No."

"Tonio! Tonio!" Robin suddenly cried.

"Shh, dear. He'll be along."

"Dare he *iss!* Dare he *iss!* Mom*ee!*" he shrieked, "Come see my fire engine, shall we?"

"Oh, thank God, thank God they're safe," said Miss Schmidt. She hugged Robin until he grunted.

"I'm all choked up," growled Mary Haunt. Again she made the angry gesture at the house. "*What* a mess. Everything I own—the war-paint, the clothes, all my magazines—everything, gone. You know what that means. I—"

I've got to go home now. And it was here, on the slightest matter of phrasing that the strange flash of silver suffused Mary Haunt; not under the descending scythe of Death, nor under the impact of soul found, heart found: just for the nudge of a word, she had her timeless instant.

All her life and the meaning of her life and all the things in it: the dimity curtains and home-baked bread, Jackie and Seth whamming away at each other for the privilege of carrying her books, the spice-shelf and the daffodils under the parlor windows. She'd loved it so, and reigned over it; and mostly, she'd been a gentle princess and ruled kindly.

Did they throw you out, gal?

She'd never known where it started, how it came about, until now. Now, with astonishment, she did. Daddy started it, before she was old enough to walk, Daddy one of the millions who had applauded a child actress called Shirley Temple, one of the thousands who had idolized her, one of the hundreds who had deified her. "Little Mary Hollywood," he'd called his daughter, and it had been "When you're in pictures, honey—" Every morning was a fountain to empty the reservoir of his dreams; every

night he filled again from the depthless well of his ambition for her.

And everyone believed him. Mom came to believe him, and her kid brother, and finally everyone in town. They had to; Daddy's unswerving, undoubting conviction overrode any alternatives, and she herself clinched it, just by being what she was, an exquisite child exquisitely groomed, who grew more beautiful (by Hollywood standards) every year. She wanted what every child wants: loving attention. She got it in fullest measure. She wanted to do what every child wants to do: gain the approval of her elders. She tried; and indeed, no other course was open to her.

Did they throw you out, gal?

Perhaps Daddy might have outgrown it; or if not, perhaps he'd have known, or found out, how to accomplish his dream in a real world. But Daddy died when she was six, and Mom took over his dream as if it had been a flower from his dead hand. She did not nourish it; she pressed it between the leaves of her treasured memories of him. It was a live thing, true, but arrested at the intensity and the formlessness of his hopes for her when she was six. She encouraged the child only to want to be in pictures, and to be sure she would be; it never occurred to her that there might be things for the child to learn. Her career was coming; it was coming like Christmas.

But no one knew when.

And when she cleaned house, they all thought it was sweet, so pretty to watch, but they'd rather take the broom away from her; and when

she baked, it was pretty too but not what she was really *for*; and when she read the diet sections in the grocery magazines, that was all right, but the other features—how to make tangerine gravy for duck, how to remove spots from synthetic fibers—"Why, Mary! you'll have a little army worrying about those things for you!"

Movie magazines then, and movies, and waiting, until the day she left.

Did they throw you out, gal?

Screen Society had a feature on Hollywood High School, and it mentioned how many stars and starlets had come from there, and the ages some of them had been when they signed contracts. And suddenly she wasn't the Shirley Temple girl at all, she was older, years older than two girls in the article, the same age as five of them. Yet here she was still, while the whole town waited . . . suppose she never made it? Suppose nothing happened here? And she began to interpret this remark, that look, the other silence, in ways that troubled her, until she wanted to hide, or to drop dead, or leave.

Just like that, leaving was the answer. She told no one, she took what clothes she had that were good, she bought a ticket for just anywhere and wrote thrilling, imaginative, untrue letters at wider and wider intervals. Naïvely she got a job which might mean her Big Break and which actually never would. And at last she reached a point where she would not look back, for wanting home so much; she would not look forward, for knowing there was nothing there; she held herself in a present of futility and pur-

posive refusal to further the ambition she insisted she had; and she had no pleasure and no
outlet but anger. She took refuge in her furies;
she scorned people and what they did and what
they wanted, and told them all so. And she took
the picture of Mom standing in front of the
house in the spring, with the jonquils all about
and the tulips coming, and she wrapped it up
in the cotton print Mom had made for her fourteenth birthday and never given her because
Screen Society had said princess-style for tee-
ners was corny.

Did they throw you out, gal?

Old Sam had asked her that; he knew, even
when she didn't. But now, in this strange silver
moment, she knew; she knew it all. Yes, they
had thrown her out. They had let her be a dead
man's dream until she was nearly dead herself.
They never let her be Mary Haunt who wanted
to fix the new curtains and bake a berry pie,
and have a square hedge along the Elm Street
side and go to meeting on Sundays. They had
marked her destiny on her face and body and
on the clothes she wore, and stamped it into her
speech and fixed her hair the way they wanted
it, and to the bottom of her heart she was angry.

And now, all of a sudden, and for the very
first time, it occurred to her that she could, if
she wanted, be Mary Haunt her own self, and
be it right there at home; that home was the
best place to be that very good thing, and she
could replace their disappointment with a very
real pride. She could be home before the Straw-
berry Festival at the church; she would wear an
apron and get suds on her forehead when she

pushed her hair back, the way Bitty did sometimes.

So Mary Haunt sat on a fire engine, next to
the high-school librarian who was enveloped in
a tremendous raincoat, saying that everything
was burned up, lost; and about to say, "I've got
to go home now." But she said, "I can go home
now." She looked into Miss Schmidt's eyes and
smiled a smile the older woman had never
seen before. "I can, I can! I can go home now!"
Mary Haunt sang. Impulsively she took Miss
Schmidt's hand and squeezed it. She looked into
her face and laughed, "I'm not mad any more,
not at you or anybody . . . and I've been a little
stinker and I'm sorry; I'm going *home!*" And
Miss Schmidt looked at the smudged face, the
scorched hair drawn back into a childish pony-
tail and held by a rubber band, the spotless
princess dress. "Why," said Miss Schmidt,
"you're beautiful, just beautiful!" "I'm not. I'm
seventeen, only seventeen," Mary Haunt said
out of a wild happiness, "and I'm going home
and bake a cake." And she hugged her mother's
picture and smiled; even the ruined house did
not glow quite this way.

EXCERPT FROM FIELD EXPEDITION [NOTEBOOK]: [! ! !]
Did it ever work! [You]'d think these specimens had used Synapse Beta sub Sixteen all
their lives! If [we] had a [tenth] as much stamina
[we] could [lie down] in a [bed] of paradoxes
and go to [sleep].
[We] will observe for a [short period] longer,
and then pack up and leave. This is a [fasci-

nating] place to visit, but [I] wouldn't want to [live] here.

XVI

It was October, and possibly the last chance they'd have for a picnic, and the day agreed and was beautiful for them. They found a fine spot where a stand of birch grew on both sides of an old split-rail fence, and a brook went by just out of sight. After they were finished O'Banion lay on his stomach in the sun, and thoughtfully scratched his upper lip with a bit of straw.

His wife laughed softly.

"Hm?"

"You're thinking about the Bittelmans again."

"How'd you know?"

"Just used to it. When you go off into yourself and look astonished and mystified and annoyed all at once, it's the Bittelmans again."

"Harmless hobby," said Halvorsen, and smiled.

"Is it, Phil? Tonio, how would you like me to go all pouty and coy and complain that you've spent more time thinking about them than about me?"

"Do by all means go all pouty and coy. I'll divorce you."

"Tony!"

"Well," he said lazily, "I had so much fun marrying you in the first place that it might be worth doing again. Where's Robin?"

"Right h—Oh, dear, *Robin!*"

Down in the cleft, where the brook gurgled,

Robin's voice answered instantly. "Frogs here, Mommy. Deelicious!"

"Does he eat 'em raw?" asked Halvorsen mildly.

Sue laughed. "That just means 'pretty' or 'desirable' or even 'bright green.' Robin, don't you dare get wet, you promise me?"

"I promise me," said the voice.

"And don't go away!"

"I don't."

"Why don't they show up?" demanded O'Banion. "Just once, that's all I'd ever want. Just show their faces and answer two questions."

"Why don't who—oh, Sam and Bitty. What two questions?"

"What they did to us, how and why."

"That's one question, counsellor?" asked Halvorsen.

"Yes. Two: What they are."

"Now, why'd you say 'what' instead of 'who'?"

"It comes to that." He rolled over and sat up. "Honey, would you mind if I ran down everything we've found out so far, just once more?"

"Summarize and rest your case?"

"I don't know about resting it . . . reviewing the brief."

"I often wonder why you call it a brief," Halvorsen chuckled.

O'Banion rose and went to the fence. Putting one hand on a slender birch trunk, he hopped upward, turning, to come to rest sitting on the top rail. "Well, one thing I'm sure of: Sam and Bitty could *do* things to people, and they did it

to all of us. And I refuse to believe that they did it with logic and persuasion."

"They could be pretty persuasive."

"It was more than that," O'Banion said impatiently. "What they did to me changed everything about me."

"How very intriguing."

"Everything about the way I *think*, hussy. I can look back on that now and realize that I was roped, thrown and notched. When he wanted me to answer questions I had to answer them, no matter what I was thinking. When he was through with me he turned me loose and made me go back to my business as if nothing had happened. Miss Schmidt told me the same thing." He shifted his weight on the rail and said excitedly, "Now there's our prize exhibit. All of us were—changed—by this thing, but Reta—she's a *really* different person."

"She wasn't more changed than the others," said Sue soberly. "She's thirty-eight years old. It's an interesting age because when you're there and look five years older, and then spruce up the way she did and look five years younger, it looked like twenty years' difference, not ten. That's all cosmetics and clothes, though. The real difference is as quiet and deep as—well, Phil here."

Again Halvorsen found a smile. "Perhaps you're right. She shifted from the library to teaching. It was a shift from surrounding herself with other people's knowledge to surrounding other people with hers. She's alive."

"I'll say. Boyfriend too."

"Quiet and deep," said O'Banion thought-

fully, swinging his feet. "That's right. All you get out of Halvorsen when you ask him about it is a smile like a light going on and, 'Now it's right for me to be me.' "

"That's it—all of it," chuckled Halvorsen happily.

"And Mary Haunt, bless her. Second happiest child I ever saw. *Robin! Are you all right?*"

"Yis!" came the voice.

"I'm still not satisfied," said O'Banion. "I have the feeling we're staring at very petty and incidental results of some very important cause. In a moment of acute stress I made a decision which affected my whole life."

"*Our.*"

He blew her a kiss. "Reta Schmidt says the same thing, though she wouldn't go into detail. And maybe that's what Halvorsen means when he says, '*Now*, it's right for me . . .' *You* annoy me."

"Sir!" she cried with mock horror.

He laughed. "You know what I mean. Only you got exposed to the Bittelmans and didn't change. Everybody else got wonderful," he smiled, "You just stayed wonderful. Now what's so special about you?"

"Must I sit here and be—"

"Shush. Think back. Was there any *different* kind of thing that happened to you that night, some kind of emergency thinking you did that was above and beyond anything you thought you could do?"

"Not that I remember."

Suddenly he brought his fist down on his thigh. "There *was!* Remember right after we got

out of the house, the wall fell on us? You dragged me back and held me still and that attic vent dropped right around us?"

"That. Yes, I remember. But it wasn't special. It just made sense."

"*Sense?* I'd like to put a computer on that job—after scorching it half through and kicking it around a while. Somehow you calculated how fast that thing was falling and how much ground it would cover when it hit. You computed that against our speed outward. You located the attic vent opening and figured where it would land, and whether or not it could contain us both. Then you estimated our speed *if* we went toward the safe spot and concluded that we could make it. *Then* you went into action, more or less over my dead body to boot. All that in—" He closed his eyes to relive the moment. "—all of one and a half seconds absolute tops. It wasn't *special?*"

"No, it wasn't," she said positively. "It was an emergency, don't you see? A real emergency, not only because we might get hurt, but in terms of all we were to each other and all we could be if only you—"

"Well, I did," he smiled. "But I still don't understand you. You mean you think more, not less—widen your scope instead of narrowing your focus when it's that kind of emergency? You can think of all those things at once, better and faster and more accurately?"

Halvorsen suddenly lunged and caught O'Banion's foot, pulling it sharply upward. He shouted "*Yoop!*" His right hand whipped up and back and scrabbled at the tree-trunk; his torso

twisted and his left hand shot straight down.
His legs flailed and straightened; for a moment
he see-sawed on the rail on his kidneys. At last
he got his left hand on the rail and pulled himself upward to sit again. "Hey! What do you
think you're—"

"Proving a point," said Halvorsen. "Look,
Tony: without warning you were thrown off balance. What did you do? You reached out for
that tree-trunk without looking—got it, too; you
knew just how fast and how far to go. But at
the same time you put your left hand straight
down, ready to catch your weight if you went
down to the ground. Meantime you banged
around with your legs and shifted your weight
this way just enough to make a new balance on
top. Now tell me: did you sit there after I
pushed you and figure all those things out, one
by one?"

"By golly no. Snop—snap—synapses."

"What?"

"Synapses. Sort of pathways in the brain that
get paved better and better as you do something
over and over. After a while they happen without
conscious thought. Keeping your balance is that
kind of thing, on the motor level. But don't tell
me you have a sort of . . . personal-cultural inner
ear—something that makes you reach reflexively
in terms of your past and your future and . . . but
that's what happened to me that night!" He stared
at Halvorsen. "You figured that out long ago, you
and your IBM head!"

"It always happens if the emergency's a bad
one," Sue said composedly. "Sometimes when
you don't even know it is an emergency. But

what's remarkable? Aren't drowning men supposed to see their whole lives pass before them?"

"Did you say that always happens with your emergencies?"

"Well, doesn't it?"

Suddenly he began to chuckle softly, and at her questioning look he said, "You remind me of something a psychologist told me once. A man was asked to describe his exact sensations on getting drunk. 'Just like anybody else,' he says 'Well, describe it,' says the doctor. The man says, 'Well, first your face gets a little flushed and your tongue gets thick, and after a while your ears begin to wiggle—' Sue, honey, I've got news for you. Maybe you react like that in important moments, a great big shiny flash of truth and proportional relationships, but believe me, other people don't. I never did until that night. *That's it!*" he yelled at the top of his voice.

From down the slope came a clear little voice, "Wash 'at noice?"

Sue and Halvorsen smiled at one another and then O'Banion said earnestly, "That's what Bitty and Sam gave us—a synaptic reflex like the equilibrium mechanisms, but bigger—much bigger. A human being is an element in a whole culture, and the culture itself is alive . . . I suppose the species could be called, as a whole, a living thing. And when we found ourselves in a stress situation which was going to affect us signally—dangerously, or just importantly—we reacted to it in the way I did just now when you pushed me—only on a cultural level. It's as if Sam and Bitty had found a way to install or

develop that 'balancing' mechanism in us. It resolved some deep personal conflict of Halvorsen's; it snapped Mary out of a dangerous delusion and Miss Schmidt out of a dangerous retreat. And, well, you know about me."

"I can't believe people don't think that way in emergencies!" she said, dazed.

"Maybe some do," said Halvorsen. "Come to think of it, people do some remarkable things under sudden stress; they make not-obvious but very right choices under pressure, like the man who cracks a joke and averts a panic or the boy who throws himself on a grenade to save his squad. They've surveyed themselves in terms of all they are and measured that against their surroundings and all it is—all in a split fraction of a second. I guess everyone has it. Some of it."

"Whatever this synapse is, the Bittelmans gave it to us . . . yes, and maybe set the house on fire too . . . why? Testing? Testing what—just us, or human beings? *What are they?*" demanded the lawyer.

"Gone, that's what," said Halvorsen.

For a very brief time, he was wrong to say that.

EXCERPT FROM FIELD EXPEDITION [NOTEBOOK]: [Our] last [hour] here, so [we] [induced] three of the test specimens to [locus B] for final informal observation. [Smith] pretends to a certain [chagrin]. After all, [he] [says] all [we] did was to come [sizable abstract number] of [terrestrially immeasurable distance unit]s, forgoing absolutely the company of [our] [   ] and the pleasures of the [   ]; strain [our] ingenuity and our [technical

equipment] to the [break]ing point, even getting trapped into using that [miserable impractical] power supply and [charge]ing it up every [month]—all to detect and analyze the incidence of Synapse Beta sub Sixteen. And here these specimens sit, locating and defining the Synapse during a brief and idle conversation! Actually, [I] [think] [Smith] is [pleased] with them for it. We shall now [dismantle] the [widget] and the [wadget] and [take off].

Robin was watching a trout.

"Tsst! Tsst!"

He was watching more than the trout, really; he was watching its shadow. It had occurred to him that perhaps the shadow wasn't a shadow, but another and fuzzier kind of fish which wouldn't let the more clear-cut one get away from over it, so maybe that was why the trout kept hanging into the current, hanging and *zoom!* darting forward. But he never was fast enough for the fuzzy one, which stayed directly under him no matter what.

"Tsst! Robin!"

He looked up, and the trout was forgotten. He filled his powerful young lungs with air and his face with joy, and then made a heroic effort and stifled his noisy delight in obedience to that familiar finger-on-lips and its explosive *"Shh!"*

Barely able to contain himself, he splashed straight across the brook, shoes and all, and threw himself into Bitty's arms. "Ah Robin!" said the woman, "wicked little boy. Are you a wicked little boy!"

"Yis. Bitty-bitty-BITTY!"

"Shh. Look who's with me." She put him down, and there stood old Sam. "Hey-y-y-y, boy?"

"Ah Sam!" Robin clasped his hands together and got them between his knees, bending almost double in delight. "Ware you *been*, Sam?"

"Around," said Sam. "Listen, Robin, we came to say goodby. We're going away now."

"Don't go 'way."

"We have to," said Bitty. She knelt and hugged him. "Goodby, darling."

"Shake," said Sam gravely.

"Shake, rattle an' roll," said Robin with equal sobriety.

"Ready, Sam?"

"All set."

Swiftly they took off their bodies, folded them neatly and put them in two small green plastic cases. On one was lettered [WIDGET] and on the other [WADGET], but of course Robin was too young to read. Besides, he had something else to astonish him. "Boff!" he cried. "Googie!"

Boff and Googie [waved] at him and he waved back. They picked up the plastic cases and threw them into a sort of bubble that was somehow there, and [walked] in after them. Then they [went].

Robin turned away and without once looking back, climbed the slope and ran to Sue. He flung himself into her lap and uttered the long, whistle-like wail that preceded his rare bouts with bitter tears.

"Why *darling*, whatever happened? What *is* it? Did you bump your—"

He raised a flushed and contorted face to her.

"Boff gone," he said wetly, "Oh, oh-h-h, Boff an' Googie gone."

He cried most of the way home, and never mentioned Boff again.

INCIDENTAL [NOTES] ON FIELD REPORT: The discovery of total incidence and random use of Synapse Beta sub Sixteen in a species is unique in the known [cosmos]; yet introduction of the mass of data taken on the Field Expedition into the [master] [computer] alters its original [dictum] not at all: the presence of this Synapse in a species ensures its survival.

In the particular case at hand, the species undoubtedly bears, and will always bear, the [curse] of interpersonal and intercultural frictions, due to the amount of paradox possible. Where so many actions, decisions, and organizational activities can occur uncontrolled by the Synapse and its [universal-interrelational] modifying effect, paradox must result. On the other [hand], any species with such a concentration of the Synapse, even in partial use, will not destroy itself and very probably cannot be destroyed by anything.

Prognosis positive.

Their young are delightful. [I] [feel good]. [Smith], [I] [forgive] [you].

THE TOR DOUBLES

Two complete short science fiction novels in one volume!